He Went With Marco Polo

Publisher's Note

He Went With Marco Polo was written over 80 years ago and tells the story of a young man accompanying Marco Polo on his adventures around the world.

An excellent storyteller, Louise Andrews Kent provides the reader with the opportunity to experience a different time and place through the eyes of the main character, including the social customs, religious beliefs, and racial relations. Taking place over 700 years ago, many parts of life are foreign and sometimes offensive to us now, including specific customs, practices, beliefs, and words. To maintain and provide historical accuracy and to allow a true representation of this time period the words used and the customs and attitudes described have not been removed or edited.

This edition published 2022
by Living Book Press

ISBN: 978-1-922634-99-3 (hardcover)
        978-1-922634-98-6 (softcover)

Copyright © 1935 by Louise Andrews Kent.

This title is published by arrangement with HarperCollins Children's Books, a division of HarperCollins Publishers. All rights reserved.

All rights reserved. No part of this publication may be reproduced, stored in a retrieval system, or transmitted in any other form or means – electronic, mechanical, photocopying, recording or otherwise, without the prior permission of the copyright owner and the publisher or as provided by Australian law.

A catalogue record for this book is available from the National Library of Australia

He Went With Marco Polo

LOUISE ANDREWS KENT

ILLUSTRATED BY

C. LEROY BALDRIDGE AND PAUL QUINN

Living Book Press

Dear Tommy:

We haven't met for a long time. The last time I saw you, we took a walk across the fields to 'Hampton.' You asked if I knew any stories. I said I knew one about a squirrel, a bad squirrel, named Bunny. So I told it, and then you said: 'Do you know any *more* stories?' So I told you one about a dog. And then you said: 'Do you know any more stories?' So I told you one about a cat.

'Don't you know any stories about *boys*?' you asked.

I said: 'My throat is tired, but I will tell you a story about a boy some other day.'

(Telling stories tires grown-up people's throats much more than talking over the telephone about how lovely the Flower Show was and 'How did you like that green dress with the mink cape?' Have you noticed that?)

'I'd like a story about *two* boys,' you said.

Well, this is a story about two boys—Marco Polo and a friend of his, Tonio Tumba. Some day perhaps you will read the book that Marco Polo wrote about his journey to Cathay. He went nearly halfway around the world and back. Not in an automobile, because he lived more than six hundred years ago. When you wanted to take a journey then, you rode on a horse, or a camel, or an elephant. Or even a donkey.

When Marco got back to Venice, where he lived, he told people all about the new places and queer people he had seen. They didn't believe him. They made fun of him. If one boy wanted to call another a liar, he would say: 'You're a regular Marco Polo!'

One word Marco often used was 'millions.' He said that Kublai Khan, the Emperor of China, had millions of people, millions of money, millions of yards of silk, and jewels worth millions. The Venetians gave Marco Polo the nickname of 'Marco Millions.' They called the place where he lived 'Millions Court'—'Corte del Millioni.' The arched doorway of Marco's house, with his coat of arms above it, is still there. So is the canal where Tonio used to row his gondola.

When Marco was very old, someone asked him if he didn't want to take back some of his big stories.

'No,' he said. 'I didn't tell half what I saw.'

It was six hundred years before people found out that Marco told the truth about China and the countries between China and Venice. There is a book six times as thick as Marco's own book and twelve times as thick as this one that tells how travellers at last discovered that Marco's stories were true.

Sir Henry Yule was the man who wrote that thick book. It helped me a great deal in making this thin one. Marco wrote his own book when he was in prison after a battle. I don't know how he liked being in prison, but anyway I'm glad he wrote the book, because if he hadn't, Tommy, your godmother—who is a little lazy about telling stories—couldn't have written this one for you.

Louise Andrews Kent

January, 1935

CONTENTS

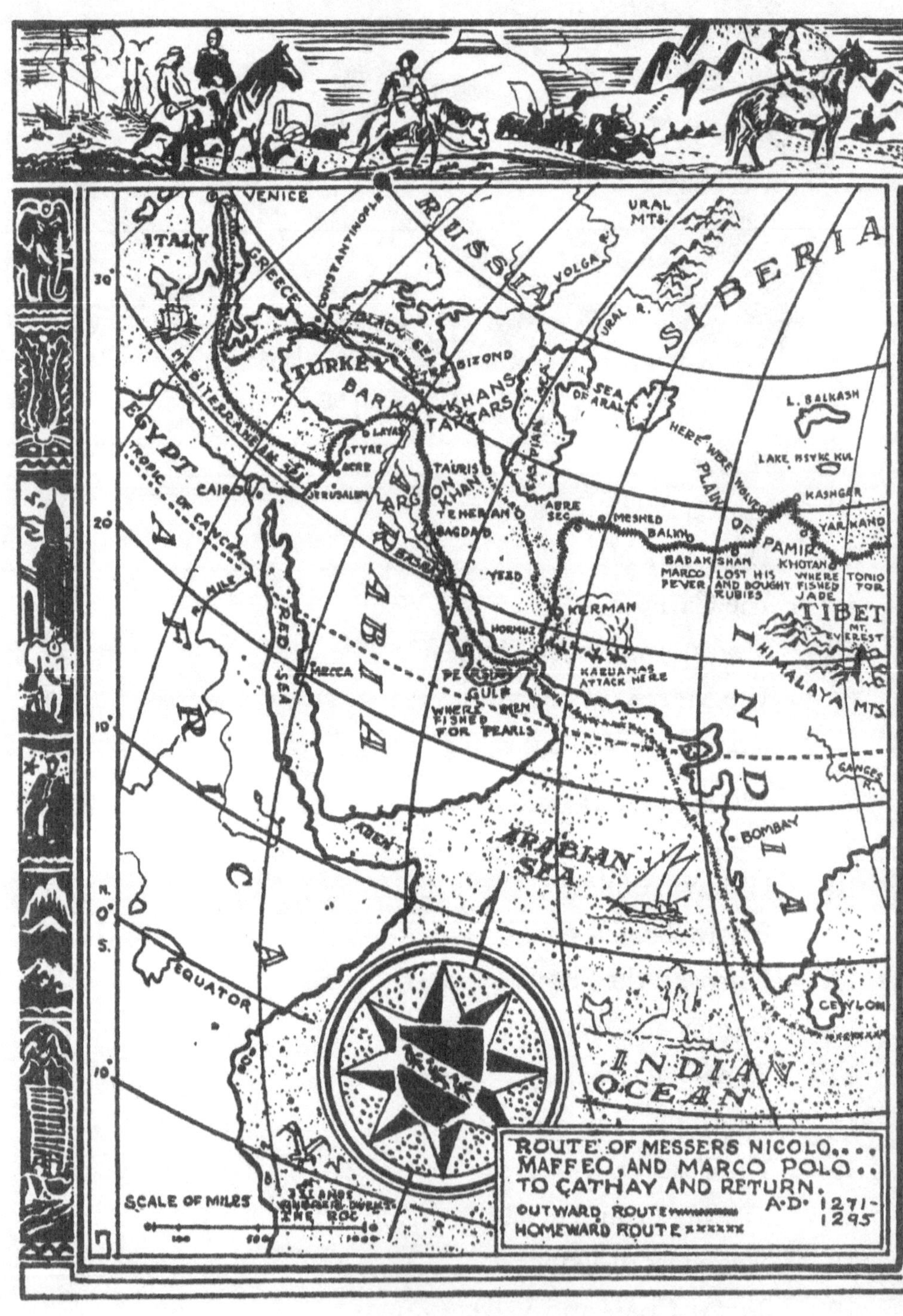
VENICE
ITALY
GREECE
CONSTANTINOPLE
RUSSIA
URAL MTS.
SIBERIA
VOLGA
URAL R.
BLACK SEA
TREBIZOND
TURKEY
BARKA KHANS
TARTARS
SEA OF ARAL
L. BALKASH
CASPIAN
HERE WERE WOLVES
LAKE ISYK KUL
MEDITERRANEAN SEA
EGYPT
TROPIC OF CANCER
CAIRO
LAYAS
TYRE
ACRE
JERUSALEM
ARGON KHAN
TAURIS
TEHERAN
BAGDAD
ABRE SEC
MESHED
PLAIN OF PAMIR
KASHGAR
YARKAND
BALKH
BADAKSHAN
MARCO FEVER
LOST HIS RUBIES
AND BOUGHT RUBIES
KHOTAN
WHERE FISHED FOR JADE
TONIO FOR JADE
ARABIA
NILE
RED SEA
AFRICA
YEZD
KERMAN
HORMUZ
TIBET
MT. EVEREST
HIMALAYA MTS.
PERSIAN GULF
CARAVANS ATTACK HERE
MECCA
WHERE MEN FISHED FOR PEARLS
INDIA
ADEN
ARABIAN SEA
GANGES R.
BOMBAY
EQUATOR
CEYLON
INDIAN OCEAN
SCALE OF MILES
ISLANDS WHERE DWELT THE ROC
100
500
1000
ROUTE OF MESSERS NICOLO,
MAFFEO, AND MARCO POLO
TO CATHAY AND RETURN.
A·D· 1271-1295
OUTWARD ROUTE
HOMEWARD ROUTE

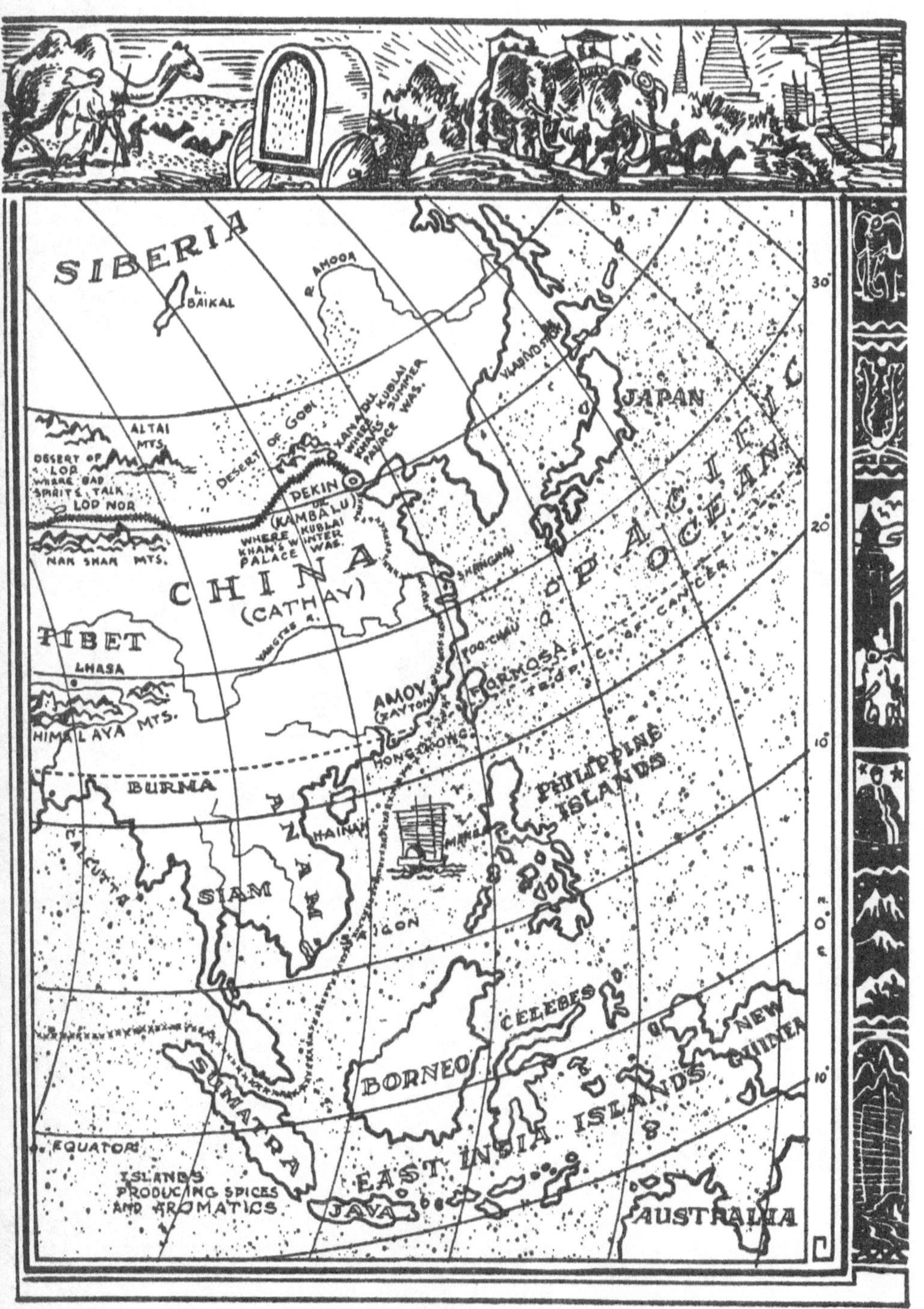

SIBERIA
L. BAIKAL
R. AMOOR
ALTAI MTS.
DESERT OF GOBI
SAINT DOLL WHERE KUBLAI KHAN'S SUMMER PALACE WAS.
DESERT OF LOP WHERE BAD SPIRITS TALK
LOD NOR
NAN SHAN MTS.
PEKIN or (KAMBALU) WHERE KUBLAI KHAN'S WINTER PALACE WAS.
VLADIVOSTOK
JAPAN
CHINA (CATHAY)
PACIFIC OCEAN
TIBET
LHASA
YANGTSE R.
SHANGHAI
HIMALAYA MTS.
FOO-CHAU
FORMOSA
TROPIC OF CANCER
AMOY (ZAYTON)
HONGKONG
BURMA
CALCUTTA
ANAM
HAINAN
MANILA
PHILIPPINE ISLANDS
SIAM
SAIGON
CELEBES
NEW GUINEA
BORNEO
SUMATRA
EAST INDIA ISLANDS
EQUATOR
ISLANDS PRODUCING SPICES AND AROMATICS
JAVA
AUSTRALIA
30
20
10
0
10

CHAPTER 1

VENICE

TONIO WAS cold—cold and very hungry. He could not remember when he had last had a proper meal. Yesterday an old woman who sold peaches near the Rialto Bridge had given him two bruised ones and he had picked up a crust of bread that someone had dropped on the quay by the gondola stand. The day before that he had caught an eel—had jumped right out of his gondola into the shallow water of the lagoon and caught it in his own hands—and had cooked it over a little fire of driftwood that he had made on the sandy beach of the Lido. Even quite a large eel is not very filling when you have had nothing else to eat and when you have to row a twenty-five-foot gondola—up and down, up and down—through long, twisting miles of canals looking for a passenger. Especially when you don't find the passenger.

Every time Tonio thought someone wanted to ride in his gondola, other gondoliers would be too quick for him. They

1

crowded him away from the gondola stand near the Doge's palace, the best stand in Venice, where his father used to work before he died. Tonio had no right there any longer, but once in a while he picked up a fare because the older gondoliers, those who had known his father, sometimes let him get in near the steps. But the new ones shoved him away. Tonio was afraid of their harsh voices and scowling faces. If one of them should ram the polished steel beak of his gondola into the faded green side of Tonio's, the boy knew that it would be the end of his boat. If it were once broken, he would never earn enough money to get it mended. And that would mean he would never be a gondolier like his father. He had had to sell his father's place at the gondola stand. On the money he got he had lived for the last year, but now it was all gone—every scudo.

Tonio had slept all night in the gondola. When the tide was low the evening before, he had pushed his boat in to a shallow channel between two banks of dark green seaweed, pulled the shabby rug over his shivering legs, put his tangled head of golden curls on a hard cushion, shut his big brown eyes, and curled up in the bottom of the boat under the tattered awning like some small animal in a burrow. At first he had been so cold he could not sleep. At last he grew warmer. The soft lapping of the water, the gentle rocking of the gondola as the tide lifted it and gurgled under it made him drowsy.

Even in his sleep he must have been listening to the water and feeling the motion of the boat, for when the tide turned and began to run out again, he woke up. It was still dark and there was a cold mist all around him, but he could feel rather than see that his floating bed was being gently carried down towards the Lido. At the Lido was the entrance through which the tide swept in and out of the canals of Venice. It was the place from which the Venetian ships sailed all over the world; the gateway through which Tonio had seen the Doge go in his galley, all shining with scarlet and gold, to drop a ring in the sea, and tell the world that Venice was the master of it.

Tonio let the gondola drift along with the tide.

'Perhaps,' he thought, 'someone off a fishing boat will want to be carried to the city. It is so early now, perhaps I shall get a fare. Perhaps some big galley came in last night. With strangers. Rich strangers who want to see the city.'

The boat drifted on a little faster. Tonio could feel the wind coming up behind him, the crisp cold wind from across the mountains that blows all the mist out to sea. In a few minutes it was clear around him. There were stars above him in the sky; more stars moving below him in the rippling water of the lagoon. The city was a dark mass behind him, with only a few small points of light low down that Tonio knew were the lamps at the gondola stands. High above it a light burned in the bell tower of San Marco.

Tonio liked that light. He always looked at it every night before he went to sleep, and the light seemed to say to him: 'Cheer up, Tonio. I'm looking at you. You'll be all right tonight.'

The light seemed to know what it was talking about, for so far Tonio had been all right, but this was the coldest and hungriest time the boy had yet known. The wind cut through his thin tunic and seemed to find every hole in his ragged hose. His clothes felt damp, and there was a hollow place inside him, a hollow place that he did not think anything would ever fill. However, he looked back at the light again and it winked at him in that friendly way.

As it did so, Tonio had an idea. Perhaps the flashing light gave it to him, but anyway it came suddenly into his head.

'I'll go down to the Church of San Nicolo,' he said to himself, speaking out loud for company. 'San Nicolo is the friend of all poor boys. I'll go and pray there and ask him to send me a passenger.'

It was beginning to grow light now. There were little patches of flame-colored cloud floating above the bell tower. The morning star slipped out of the pink sky. Someone put out the big lamp in the tower. It gave Tonio one last encouraging wink. Then the tower and the domes and turrets below it were black against the sunrise.

Tonio mounted into his place at the stern of the gondola, put his heel into the heel-plate, turned out his toes as a gondolier should, and began to swing away at the heavy oar. It felt lighter than usual, for the tide and wind helped him. The gondola slid quietly through the pink-and-silver water.

Inside the Church of San Nicolo it was dark, except for the few candles burning low here and there. One of them threw its dim light on the picture of the Saint near the altar. He was a big, kind-looking man with a brown beard and a coarse brown robe. Tonio knelt down in front of the picture, and said his prayers, just the way his father had taught him to say them—all the prayers he knew. Then in his own words he said a prayer for his father and one for his mother. She had died so long ago that all Tonio knew about her was that she had come from the North and had golden hair like his own. Last of all he said the prayer for himself:

'Please, San Nicolo, I know you're good to poor boys—please help me today to go where I can find a passenger. I am so hungry.'

It did not sound much like the prayers his father had taught him, but Tonio felt better when he had said it. The Saint looked kindly down at him. The candle flared up and went out. In the last flash of light Tonio almost thought there was a smile on the brown face, a twinkle in the blue eyes, and that San Nicolo's big hand moved a little. Then the candle went out. There was a waxy smell, and a little blue smoke drifted across the picture. Tonio could hardly see the Saint now in the dim light.

'Did you point to the harbor, San Nicolo? Or the city?' murmured Tonio, but the Saint only looked past him into the shadowy church.

Tonio rowed towards the docks. There were boats of all shapes and sizes there, with brilliant sails—yellow, orange, red—shining against the rippling blue water. The sun was up now, but the wind was still cold. Everything seemed to stand out with unusual clearness—every rope of the fishing boats, every scale on every fish, every grain of yellow sand on the beach, every tiny silver ripple on the water, every sharp peak of the mountains. The men at the docks moved more quickly than usual with their kegs and baskets. Their laughing and singing seemed to ring over the shining water.

Suddenly Tonio heard a shout, then more shouts. Men, all talking at once, were running towards the side of the dock that he could not see. A man in a rowboat, just ahead of Tonio, began to row hard and in a moment disappeared around the dock. Tonio followed him as fast as he could. He buzzed the gondola along through the water, forgetting his tired arms and empty stomach, and made it swoop around the end of the dock ahead of the rowboat.

Out in the open water of the Adriatic he saw the cause of the excitement, a big galley coming up against the wind. The sun winked on the dripping oars, her bow cut through the frothing caps of the waves, flags fluttered from her masts. As she turned to come alongside the dock, Tonio saw that one of the flags was one he had often seen before—the red flag of Venice with the gold lion of San Marco on it. There was another red flag, too, with a wide gold stripe going from one corner of it to the other and three black birds on the gold stripe. Somewhere he thought he had seen it. The birds were starlings. A starling was a 'Polo' in Tonio's language. He had heard of a family named Polo. Perhaps the flag was theirs.

Tonio went to a small wharf, where he moored his gondola, then hurried towards the big dock. Men were already landing from the galley and there was the usual noise and chatter going on. In fact there was rather more than the usual noise. Most of it seemed to be centred around two men in brown robes of a cut strange to Tonio, men with bushy beards and bronzed faces. People were slapping them on the back and making much more fuss over them than over the more brightly dressed men who were still streaming off the ship. Tonio saw the admiral of the fleet himself, in his scarlet satin doublet and violet cap, taking the taller of the two bearded men by the shoulders and giving him a friendly shake.

The porters began unloading the cargo. By his nose Tonio could tell that this ship was from the East, for he could smell all kinds of spicy smells—cinnamon, mace, pepper, cloves. The fragrance hung around the ship and everything in it. Even the bas-kets of figs, the kegs of honey, the sacks of almonds had a breath of the Far East about them. Tonio would have liked to stay until the last bale of silk or cotton was unloaded,

but he saw gondoliers and other boatmen arriving and heard men from the galley bargaining for the trip to the city. He knew that if he were ever going to get a passenger, this was the time. He would have liked to speak to one of the big men in the brown robes—the taller had about him something that reminded Tonio of the kind face of San Nicolo in the picture—but they were still the centre of a talking, laughing group. The other men who were coming off the galley looked too proud and too gaily dressed. Tonio wished he had been able to make himself look better. He had run his fingers through his untidy curls, and washed his face in the half-salty water of the lagoon. His skin felt sticky, and he knew by his reflection in the water—the only mirror he had—that he looked shabby and rumpled.

'I am dirty and my boat is dingy,' thought Tonio. 'All the other gondoliers look so grand and their gondolas shine like the sun and the sea. Of course no one will hire me.'

Just then his eye fell on a man who was standing a little outside the noisy group, a short, round-faced man with a moustache the color of straw drooping over a thin, straw-colored beard. He was looking at the laughing men out of a pair of gentle, pale blue eyes. No one was paying any attention to him. He was shabbily dressed in faded blue cloth, stained with sea-water and patched with squares of various colors here and there. He had a queer straw hat on his lanky, straw-colored hair. On his feet were scarlet leather boots, much too big for him, and pulled on over blue hose as ragged as Tonio's. The boots were splendidly stamped with gold patterns of vines and flowers. They were so gay that they made the rest of the man's costume look all the dingier. Beside him was a big bag made of a cow's hide with the hair still on. It had leather cord run through slits in the top of it. The man had his hand pushed through a loop in the cord. Every now and then he walked a step or two, still looking patiently at the jolly group. Every time he took a step, the bag moved a little and things clinked inside it. At last he spoke softly to one of the men in the brown robes, the short fat one with the curly black beard.

The fat man bellowed cheerfully:

'Go on, then, Hans. We'll see you later. Take care of my bag,' and he turned back to his friends. 'Don't believe me if you don't want to,' Tonio heard him say. 'It's nothing to me. But I tell you this Khan is so great that lions and elephants bow before him. And the beggars in Cathay wear silk...'

The man with the scarlet boots smiled. When he smiled he looked so kind that Tonio felt brave enough to speak to him.

'I have my gondola here, sir, if you would like to go to the city.'

The man smiled again and looked at Tonio out of his kind blue eyes.

'The bag is not light,' he said in a gentle voice, speaking slowly, as if he had to hunt for the words. 'You think your arms are strong enough? You are not very big.'

Then, seeing the look of disappointment on Tonio's face, he added hastily: 'But then I am not so big either. Come, then, where is this fine boat?'

He would not let Tonio take his bag, but walked after him in his scarlet boots with the clinking, hairy sack thrown over his shoulder.

It was hard work rowing the gondola back to the city—tide and wind were both against them—but Tonio managed it, in spite of his tired arms and the empty place inside him. He began to think what he would have for breakfast—a hot, crusty loaf of bread from the bakery in the Piazzetta, hot roasted chestnuts, perhaps, and sausages sizzling and spitting in the pan at the cookshop. No eels. Anyone who wanted eels was welcome to them!

There was the smell of new baked bread blowing across the Piazzetta from the bakery as Tonio slid his gondola skillfully along the steps and sprang out to help his passenger. The little man took out of a leather pouch that was hung at his belt a handful of silver coins and a piece of yellow paper. Tonio had never seen a piece like it. There was strange-looking writing on it, and a scarlet seal. Tonio's father had taught him to read a little, but he had never seen writing like that on the yellow paper.

Hans of the Scarlet Boots—that was the name Tonio had given his passenger—held out both hands, the silver coins in his right hand and the yellow paper in his left.

'Which will you have, left or right?' he said, smiling at Tonio out of his kind blue eyes. 'That yellow topknot of yours makes me homesick'—he jerked his head towards the mountains to the north. 'I want to pay you well for the trip. Take whichever you like.'

'I'll take a silver piece, thank you,' said Tonio. He really could have sausages, he knew now, and all the bread he wanted.

The little man smiled again and poured all the silver into Tonio's thin hand.

'Take it, then,' he said, patting the boy on the shoulder. 'And if you should ever go to Cathay, don't tell my friend Kublai Khan that you took a handful of Venice groats rather than his money that's worth a hundred golden ducats! Well, I see I'll have to go back to Cathay to spend it.'

He smiled again at Tonio, crammed the yellow paper back into his pouch, shouldered his clinking bag, and strolled off towards the Doge's palace.

Tonio wondered who Kublai Khan was.

'Cathay,' he said to himself—'Cathay. I never heard of it. It must be a long way off.'

CHAPTER 2

MARCO POLO'S GONDOLIER

IT DID not take Tonio long to turn one of his silver groats into food.

'This is a lucky morning,' he thought. 'Tomorrow I will take a fat candle to San Nicolo and light it for him, so that he will know I am grateful.'

But San Nicolo was not through with Tonio.

Crossing the square towards the gondola stand were two boys, one a little older than Tonio—fifteen, perhaps—one several years younger. The older boy had a sensible face, keen gray eyes, rather a long nose, a wide, firm mouth, stiff, curly brown hair. He looked strong and wise, Tonio thought. His shoulders were broad, his legs sturdy. Everything about him—the swing of his crimson cloak, the firm way he had of walking, the quick turn of his head, the gleam of his gray eyes—made Tonio wish that he knew him. The other boy was delicate-looking, almost pretty, with his plump pink-and-white face, soft curls, and blue eyes. His legs were short, and he could not have kept up with the older boy without hurrying if the older one—Tonio was sure they were brothers, for their eyes were alike in spite of the difference in color—had not walked slowly.

A servant behind them was carrying an enormous basket out of which stuck the yellow legs of several fowls. There were cabbages and onions in the basket, too, and a big melon. The older boy had a basket of peaches in his hand. The younger one was eating a peach; some of the juice ran down his chin.

'Maffeo,' groaned the other boy, 'if you get peach juice on your new doublet, what will Aunt Bella say?'

The pink-faced boy hastily rubbed his chin with the back of his hand. He was more handsomely dressed than his brother in a tunic of blue with gold threads woven in it, making patterns of birds and flowers. His cloak was a blue velvet with a scarlet lining. He had on a scarlet velvet cap with a white feather in it and thin blue shoes with scarlet edges. The older boy produced a piece of linen and gave his brother's face a scrub. Maffeo wriggled away.

'Let me go, Marco,' he said. 'You're as bad as a dozen aunts yourself.'

He smiled as he said it and his brother smiled back at him.

They looked so jolly that Tonio thought he would speak to them. He felt bolder now that he had eaten and that he had already had one passenger.

'If you need a gondola, sir,' he said politely to the older brother, 'mine is at the steps there near the columns. It is only a shabby one,' Tonio added, 'but it is dry and I can take you quickly.'

'Is it your own?' asked Maffeo, snatching another peach out

of the basket, and bending over carefully so that the juice fell on the pavement this time.

'It was my father's,' said Tonio, 'but now it is mine.'

The older boy looked at him kindly. Probably this keen-looking boy understood why Tonio's hair was so tangled and his clothes so shabby.

'We'll go in his gondola, shall we, Maffeo?' the boy said, and gave Tonio the basket of peaches.

Tonio trotted off towards the place where he had moored the green gondola. He was beginning to feel a little uneasy, for the painted pole to which he had tied his boat belonged to the Traghetto—the gondola stand. However, it was still so early that he hoped that his gondola would not be in anyone's way. His arms and legs had new strength in them. He swung the basket around his head gaily, peaches and all. Maffeo whooped delightedly behind him. Tonio ran on happily.

But he had stayed away too long. Coming up the steps from the canal was the gondolier who had bought Tonio's father's place at the gondola stand. Tonio had always been afraid of the fat, yellow-faced Luigi Rosso. He felt more than ever frightened as he saw that the fat gondolier's hard black eyes were fixed on him.

Luigi walked to the post where Tonio had moored the shabby green gondola. Luigi's own gondola, a handsome black-and-gold boat, with the sunshine winking on its polished steel beak, the wind fluttering its purple-and-gold awning, lay beside the steps. Luigi unfastened the knot in Tonio's rope. He looked over his shoulder with a smile that made Tonio very uncomfortable. Tonio hurried forward. He arrived at the post just as Luigi, who had unknotted the rope, gave the green gondola a push with his foot and began to pull his own gondola in towards the steps.

Tonio jumped, basket of peaches and all, and by good luck landed on the bow of the green gondola. He said nothing to Luigi, who stood scowling at him, but only set down the basket and hurried to the stern of his own boat.

The two brothers were at the steps now and Tonio tried to work his boat over near them, but the black gondola blocked the way. Luigi got into it.

He gave a short laugh and turned towards Tonio's passengers.

'My gondola is at your service, gentlemen,' he said in his smooth, fat voice.

'We've engaged someone already,' said the older boy. 'Move away, please, and let him come up to the steps.'

'Oh,' said Luigi, still in his smooth voice, 'so I should move my beautiful boat away and let that little thief come up in his rotten green pea-pod! I don't think the gentleman understands the rules of the Traghetto.'

'I understand a mean trick when I see one,' said the boy called Marco. 'Get out of the way, please.'

Luigi was no longer looking at Tonio. His voice got louder and less smooth. He began to say things—cruel things, mean things—about Tonio and Tonio's father, but he looked at the sturdy boy in the red cloak.

The stern of the black gondola had floated out a little from the steps. Tonio pushed the nose of the green one in behind it, gently, so that Luigi did not feel the motion. Tonio was almost alongside the steps when Luigi turned his head.

The fat gondolier gave an angry roar, ran down to the end of his boat, straddled the water between the two gondolas and began to hit Tonio with his plump fists. In a moment he had both feet in the green gondola and was shaking Tonio by the neck over the water.

Tonio kicked and squirmed, but he was helpless in Luigi's grasp. Then suddenly the fat gondolier let him go. Tonio would have fallen into the water if he had not managed to grasp his oar. He felt his gondola rocking violently and thumping against the stone steps. Tonio opened his eyes and saw that now Luigi was being held over the water by the neck. The boy in the red cloak had hold of Luigi's collar and was shaking him far harder than Tonio had been shaken. Tonio jumped down towards the struggling figures. He got hold of one of Luigi's ankles and pushed it over the side of the boat. The boy in the red cloak gave a heave. The fat gondolier disappeared with a splash in the green water. Tonio saw that as Luigi fell his head grazed against the steel beak of the black gondola. In a moment the fat, yellow face came up above the water. Blood began to run down his cheek from an ugly curved cut just below his eye.

The boy in the red cloak said: 'Oh, he's hurt. That's bad!'

He and Tonio hauled the soaked and whimpering gondolier out of the water and laid him on the stones in the sunshine. People began to crowd around them.

Tonio saw walking towards them an old man, with a red velvet cap with a horn curving up at the back of it, and a black cloak wrapped around him. He had a smooth-shaven, thin face with deep creases in it. He was the Doge, the ruler of Venice. Tonio knew him by the cap. He walked slowly in scarlet slippers. After the slippers came a pair of scarlet boots. Tonio, bending over Luigi, did not have to look up to see who was wearing the boots. He saw the edges of two coarse brown robes too, and the brown leather boots of soldiers, and Maffeo's blue shoes, and the feet of gondoliers. He heard angry voices.

The Doge said: 'What's this? What's this?' And Tonio heard

the boy named Marco explaining how the accident happened. He spoke clearly and his voice sounded brave and honest.

Tonio looked up from where he was kneeling.

The boy in the crimson cloak was standing up very straight with his curly brown head thrown back, his clear gray eyes fixed on the old man in the pointed cap. Tonio stood up too, and the other boy put one of his strong hands on Tonio's thin shoulder and went on speaking.

Tonio looked at the faces. No one was looking at him. The two sunburned men with the shaggy beards whom he had seen at the Lido, Hans with the pale blue eyes and the grand red boots, the tall, wrinkled old Doge, the red-faced soldiers, even the gondoliers, were all looking at the speaker.

Marco finished what he had to say with a little bow and was silent.

The Doge turned his head towards the soldiers. There was a jewelled band around his cap. The stones flashed in the sunlight.

'Pick him up and take him to the hospital,' he said, pointing to Luigi, who still lay whining, the blood oozing out of the S-shaped cut and running down over his fat cheek into his ear. 'There seems to have been fault on both sides,' he added. 'I think, young sir, you will have to pay for having that cheek mended. As for you, boy,' he said, looking at Tonio with his tired dark eyes, 'what are we going to do with you? We can't have fighting outside our palace every morning. How shall I stop it?'

Tonio muttered that he was sorry. There would be no more fighting, he said in a low voice.

'How can I be sure of that?' asked the Doge. 'Is there anyone who will speak for you? Anyone who will bind himself to keep you in order, my young dolphin?'

He did not smile, but his voice sounded friendly.

Tonio shook his tousled yellow head sadly, but as he did so that other voice, with its frank, honest ring, said rather loud in his ear:

'*I* will bind myself, sir. I promise to look after him.'

The tall man smiled this time. In fact, he even chuckled a little.

'And who are you,' he asked, 'who make such fine promises? I thought I knew all the noble councillors and wise merchants of Venice. Have I overlooked your name in the Book of Gold, you young rooster? Crow a little more and tell it to us.

The tall boy threw his brown head back again. He looked frankly into the old man's sunken eyes and said in his ringing voice:

'You will find my father's name written there, Sir Doge, although he has been gone from Venice since I was six years old. My brother Maffeo here, he has never seen.'

Tonio saw the two men in the brown robes turn and stare at the speaker. The tall one moved forward a step, but the black-bearded one held him by the arm.

The boy went on: 'I hope you will find my name written in your Golden Book some day, sir. It is Marco Polo.'

No one spoke in the Piazzetta for a moment. Tonio heard pigeons fluttering around the columns where San Marco's lion looked crossly out over the lagoon. Then the tall man in the brown robe said, 'Marco, my son,' and the fat man with the black beard bellowed cheerfully, 'And my namesake, Maffeo,' and clapped the pink-faced boy so hard on the shoulder that he dropped his fourth peach.

Tonio turned away. He thought perhaps Marco Polo would rather greet his father without people staring at him. Tonio looked out across the rippling silver water for a minute. Then he looked down at his gondola. There were new scratches and bumps on its side where it had banged against the steps—Tonio was glad his father could not see the battered boat. He got into it and started to push off when he heard Marco Polo's voice calling to him.

'Here! Where are you going in such a hurry?'

Tonio said: 'I thought you wouldn't need me now.'

'I engaged you, didn't I?' Marco said, with a smile. 'My uncle and I will come with you. My brother will go in my father's boat.'

The fat man with the black beard jumped down into the gondola. It swished up and down in the water under his weight. Marco's father and Hans of the red boots and the pink-faced Maffeo got into another gondola.

'Beat them now! See who gets to San Felice first,' said Marco.

'San Felice,' groaned the fat man loudly. 'Do we still live in that mud hole?'

'Yes, Uncle Maffeo,' said Marco.

'And in the same house? That miserable little seagull's nest? A house you couldn't swing an eel in comfortably?'

'The same house we've always lived in. Yes, Uncle Maffeo. But I haven't tried swinging any eels in it,' said Marco gravely.

'And who lives there now?' Messer Maffeo Polo's voice echoed loudly from the houses along the canal.

'Why, just the family, my Aunt Marta and my Uncle Marco— only he's away just now—and their two children, Nicco and little Maraca,' Marco answered.

'Well, that's six of you. A nice little family,' said the fat man.

'And,' went on Marco, 'there's my Uncle Jordano Trevisan'— Uncle Maffeo groaned—'my mother's brother, you know, and his wife Fiordelisa. Aunt Lisa we call her.'

'Stop! Stop!' groaned the fat man.

'And then your cousin Felix Polo and his wife and three children. And her brother Vanni. The children are all imps. Rosa is the worst. She's the oldest. Oh, and your sister, of course, my Aunt Bella.'

Uncle Maffeo said in a hollow voice, 'How well I know it.'

'And that's all except the servants,' said Marco.

'And how many of them are there?'

'Oh, ten or a dozen—I forget which,' said Marco. 'My Aunt Bella is always getting new ones. She discharged both gondoliers yesterday. This is the new one,' he added. 'She told me to engage one.'

He smiled up at Tonio, who almost ran the gondola into the side of the narrow canal through which they were passing. He was not sure whether or not Marco Polo was joking.

He did not look as if he were, and he had promised the Doge to look after Tonio. Tonio sent the gondola flying along at its swiftest, shouting, 'Premé' and 'Stalé,' as he turned and twisted the boat around corners, as loudly as the biggest and strongest gondoliers in Venice.

THE GULL'S NEST

BUT TONIO did not reach the Polos' house first. He took a wrong turning and went through an extra length of dark canal, with houses almost touching each other and only a patch of blue sky between them. When the green gondola reached what Uncle Maffeo called the gull's nest on the mud bank, the other gondola had already arrived and the whole family was in the courtyard talking to Marco's father. Tonio thought the house was rather large for a gull's nest. It was an old house with a high tower above the doorway, and with a good deal of plaster chipped off, showing the red bricks underneath, but it looked comfortable enough to Tonio. A good deal better to sleep in than a gondola these cold nights!

The courtyard was full of people—evidently all those Marco had named and plenty of others too. Tonio followed Marco and his uncle into the court. At first no one paid any attention to them. Everyone was gathered around Messer Nicolo Polo's tall figure. Nicolo was the name of Marco's father.

'He looks like San Nicolo,' thought Tonio. 'I will take the Saint *two* candles.'

'Ha!' grumbled Uncle Maffeo. 'So this is the family. How cosy it is! Just like a caravanserai! Everyone from everywhere lives with us, I see. Only when we camp with the caravans we don't have women chattering,' he added gloomily.

The women were certainly making a good deal of noise. A very tall one in purple damask seemed to be making the most. She had a long nose and a chin that moved so fast under it that Tonio stared, wondering how she worked it.

Suddenly her eye fell on Uncle Maffeo. She pushed her way out of the group around her and swept over to where he was standing.

'Maffeo Polo,' she said in a harsh voice, 'where have you been all these years?'

Tonio expected that Uncle Maffeo would bellow his answer. He was much surprised when the jolly fat man said meekly:

'Why, my dear Bella, I have been to Cathay.'

'Cathay! That's what Nicolo says! I never heard of it. Where is it?'

Uncle Maffeo waved his fat hand rather timidly towards the east.

'Well, my dear sister, it's in that general direction. But quite a distance. Quite a distance! In fact it took us three years to get there.'

'Humph! Did you walk on your heads? And it took you three years to get back, I suppose!'

'Why, yes,' said Uncle Maffeo mildly. 'It snowed, you see. And the rivers were flooded. And then there were wars going

on. And we had to cross deserts, you know, and nearly broil—
that is, when we weren't crossing mountains and freezing.
Now, would you believe it, my dear Bella; but we travelled on
a high plain where it was so cold that we had to rub the horses'
gums with garlic, so they could breathe? And when we lighted
a fire it fluttered around so that the water boiled, but wasn't
hot enough to cook our rice?'

'I certainly wouldn't believe it. Cold boiling water indeed!'
said Aunt Bella sharply. 'And besides, that doesn't explain what
you did with the other three years. You've been gone nine years,
you know. "Just a short trip to Constantinople to sell some
soap and a cargo of Venetian glass and to buy a little silk and
indigo," you said. And then you disappear for nine years, and
leave me to take care of everything. A nice way to do!'

'Why, the other three years we were visiting Kublai Khan
in Cathay. The greatest king in the world,' said Uncle Maffeo,
still in his meek voice.

'A Christian king?' asked Aunt Bella severely.

'Well, not exactly. He's a Tartar. The Lord of all the Tartars.
But he would like to be a Christian. As a matter of fact he sent
us back with a message to the Pope to ask the Pope to send
his priests to Cathay so Kublai Khan and his people can learn
about our religion,' explained Uncle Maffeo.

'Tartars!' sniffed Aunt Bella disgustedly. 'Heathen savages, I
know all about them. So that's what you've been doing. Living
with savages. Greatest king in the world! Humph!'

Uncle Maffeo had been patient up to this moment, but now
he began to bellow again.

'Look here,' he said, 'if you don't believe he's a great king—
greater than any king—an emperor really!—how do you suppose we travelled thousands of miles safely? Found horses and

camels and donkeys whenever we needed them. Food. Soldiers to guide us. Every-thing we needed, I tell you. Look here!'

He pulled something out of the folds of his brown robe. The sunlight winked on its yellow surface.

It was a metal tablet, half as long as Tonio's arm. On one side were lines of letters like those Tonio had seen on the yellow paper that morning. On the other a picture of a hawk. A hawk with his wings outspread, his claws ready to snatch what-ever came in his way. There was a hole  through the top of the tablet through which ran a chain of gold that hung around Uncle Maffeo's fat neck.

The people in the courtyard had been gradually edging over towards Uncle Maffeo and his affectionate sister. A gasp from everyone went up as the fat traveller held up the tablet. Even Aunt Bella seemed impressed by the sight of so much gold all in one piece.

'I don't suppose it's solid,' she remarked, taking hold of it and weighing it in her skinny hand.

'Yes, it is, too, solid,' bellowed her brother, 'and it's worth more than its weight in gold. Wherever we went among the Tartars we had only to show our tablets—Nicolo has one too—and they'd give us whatever we ordered. So what do you think of a king whose people three thousand miles away will obey him if they see the picture of his hawk on a piece of metal?'

Aunt Bella seemed somewhat gladder to see her brother now.

'What I think, my dear Maffeo,' she screeched, throwing her skinny arms around her brother's plump neck, 'is that we are all delighted to see you home, and we had all better have something to eat.'

'A splendid idea,' panted Uncle Maffeo, releasing himself from his sister's grasp.

The whole crowd in the courtyard began to troop into the house. No one paid any attention to Tonio. Marco Polo's father put his arm around his tall son's shoulder and walked off with him in silence. Nicolo Polo seemed quite content to leave the talking to his brother and sister. His face looked sad. Tonio learned afterwards that Messer Nicolo had only just heard that his wife had died while he was on his long journey to Cathay.

In a few moments Tonio was alone in the courtyard. He did not know quite what to do, but it was sunny there. Pigeons were gurgling and chuckling on the window-sills. There was a smell of chickens being cooked and cakes baking. Tonio sat down in a corner against a sunny wall and went to sleep.

He had no idea how long he had been dozing and dreaming when he felt himself being shaken by the shoulder. He jumped up, thinking for a moment that Luigi was going to throw him into the canal. Then he saw Marco Polo's face bending over him.

'I'm sorry I forgot you,' Marco said, with a smile, 'but this is a pretty exciting morning for me, as you may guess. We need help waiting on the table. Will you come?'

Tonio pushed the hair out of his eyes.

'In these clothes?' he asked, pointing to his ragged hose and tunic.

'I'll fix that,' said Marco. 'The last gondolier was about your size. Aunt Bella tore his clothes off him before he went, I think. Anyway, they're still here.'

Tonio was not quite sure whether it was all part of a dream; that perhaps he would wake up and find himself, after all, still in his gondola among the seaweed. If it was a dream, the crimson tunic with the Polo coat of arms embroidered on it in black and gold was warmer than clothes are in most dreams. The sleeves came down over his hands. The long black hose wrinkled, and the crimson shoes flopped, but Tonio didn't care. He thought they were splendid.

Before long he found himself clean, his golden hair combed and smooth, helping the other servants to pass delicious-smelling dishes to the guests that were seated around the long tables.

The room was not a very large one, or perhaps it had too many people in it. The benches were crowded. Small boys and girls were jammed in between their parents. Elbows joggled each other. The tables were loaded with more silver and gold and glass, more dishes of roasted meat, more bowls of fruit, more plates of sweetmeats, than Tonio had ever seen in his whole life. He had never smelled such steaming clouds of hot spiced air as blew out of the big kitchen, never heard such spitting and sizzling of roasting ducks and geese and chickens, never felt such a thick carpet beneath his feet, never heard so much noise in so small a space. It all made Tonio feel dizzy. He slipped about in the new shoes that his toes did not fill. The bowl of gravy he was carrying kept tipping. The silver bowl was so hot that Tonio could hardly hold it, but he felt cold shivers running down his back. Sup-

pose he spilled it on that wonderful carpet! What would Aunt Bella do then?

Marco Polo nodded to him kindly from across the table and Tonio carried the hot bowl around to him. Marco was sitting between the lady in purple with the long nose and a fat little girl with brown curls and velvety brown eyes.

'Humph, who is this?' Aunt Bella said gruffly, looking at Tonio.

'The new gondolier, Aunt Bella,' answered Marco.

'H'm. Couldn't you get a bigger one? He doesn't fit the clothes very well,' said Aunt Bella, looking at the black hose that sagged around Tonio's thin legs. 'You could put two of his size in there.'

Nicolo Polo from across the table said kindly: 'He's tall enough, Bella. With all the good things you give him to eat, he'll surely fill them out before long.'

Aunt Bella said, a little more pleasantly: 'You may be right, Nicolo. What's your name, straw head?'

'Antonio Tumba, my lady,' said Tonio, bowing his yellow head and holding on to the hot bowl carefully.

Aunt Bella gave a cackling laugh.

'Tonio Tumba! Tonio Tumba! What it sounds like is a trumpet and a drum playing together. Well, it will be an easy name to call.'

She repeated the name again. A little boy tucked in between two larger ones said it over twice. His brother took it up. In a minute the whole room was chanting, 'Tonio Tumba! Tonio Tumba!' while poor Tonio stood blushing, his fingers feeling as if they were going to burn off.

'Set that gravy down,' said Aunt Bella. 'You'll be spilling it on your tunic next.'

Tonio set it down only too gladly. The little brown-eyed girl next to Marco pinched Tonio's leg and chuckled 'Tonio Tumba.' Tonio stood as still as he could.

'Stop it, Rosa,' said Marco.

'What were you doing, Rosa?' asked a plump lady farther down the table.

Tonio decided she must be Rosa's mother. She had the same soft brown eyes and curly brown hair.

Rosa glanced sidewise at Aunt Bella's stern face and then said clearly: 'I was pinching that boy under the table, Mamma.'

Aunt Bella grunted.

'When I was a little girl,' she said, 'I should have been severely punished for doing such a thing. What are the children coming to in these days!'

Rosa's mother said gently: 'I'm sure she won't do it again, Bella. Rosa is always a good girl.'

Rosa did not pinch Tonio again—that day. The next time he came past her, she tickled him, instead, in the ribs. She looked as sweet as an angel. Tonio wished she would act more like one. He was glad when Aunt Bella said crossly:

'Now go and get yourself something to eat. Don't let me see you in here again looking like a half-starved chicken.'

Tonio pulled himself away from Rosa's small tickling fingers and went back to the kitchen with his name still echoing in his ears. The meal was almost over now and the servants were eating. The cook tore off most of the side of a duck and shoved it across the table to Tonio. The young gondolier ate it carefully without getting any spots on his clothes, for Aunt Bella's sharp gray eyes to see.

When Tonio went back into the dining-hall, Messer Maffeo was standing up on a bench delivering a speech. He was telling wonderful things about Cathay, of palaces with gold on the walls, of cities with a thousand bridges all of stone—'none of these rickety wooden bridges you have in Venice, but stone bridges a mile long with a lion's head carved on every post.' He told of strange animals and birds—pheasants with tails longer than a man's arm and colored like twenty rainbows, a beast like a lion but with a mean face and striped orange, black, and white.

All the time he was talking, people laughed.

'Travellers' tales! Travellers' tales!' they called. 'Make up some more stories, Maffeo.'

'You don't believe me!' roared Messer Maffeo. 'Hans—where is Hans? Bring me my bag, Hans.'

The little man with the red boots had been sitting quietly at a table in a corner of the room with some of the younger children and their nurses. He got up now and came forward, dragging behind him the cowhide bag that Tonio had noticed that morning. It still clinked as Hans moved.

Maffeo Polo heaved the bag up onto the end of the table.

He began to pull things out of it and toss them along the table: bracelets rough with blue turquoises, a cup and saucer of scarlet lacquer, a tree carved out of green jade, ivory elephants, ivory monkeys, ivory camels; balls of carved ivory with other balls inside them.

A scarlet leather whip with a gold handle landed in front of Marco's place. A necklace of gold and pearls at Aunt Bella's. Little Rosa got a fan of feathers. She tickled Tonio's nose with it when he came past with a bowl of almonds.

'Of course she *would* get something she could tickle me with!' Tonio thought.

There seemed to be no bottom to the bag. Uncle Maffeo tossed ribbons and pieces of gold-embroidered silk to the ladies, knives with jewelled handles to the men, ivory animals to the children. Even Tonio found himself with an ivory elephant in his hand.

'And that,' said Uncle Maffeo, 'is the way we do in Cathay.'

THE CA' POLO

'THIS MORNING,' said Uncle Maffeo to Tonio, 'we'll go house-hunting. Don't tell.'

He winked at Tonio and spoke in what he meant for a whisper, but it was really a gentle roar. Fortunately there was no one else on the steps where the green gondola stood ready.

Tonio had lived with the Polo family now for several weeks. The green gondola had been freshly painted. It had touches of gold on it here and there. The brass dolphins that held the oar shone like gold. The steel beak was polished so that it was as bright as silver. The gondola had a new awning of red-and-gold. A red flag with the three black 'Poli' on a broad band of gold flapped above the shining beak.

Tonio in his red-and-black clothes jumped to his place at the oar. He was beginning to fill out his new stockings. His hair shone in the sunshine, like the brass dolphins and like the wide gold band of the Polo coat of arms.

Messer Nicolo Polo followed his brother into the gondola. He smiled kindly at Tonio. Tonio liked the big quiet man who looked so much like the picture of San Nicolo. In fact it was hard to tell which of the Polo family he liked best. He did not mind Rosa's sly pinchings and ticklings. He thought everything Marco did was perfect. He even liked Aunt Bella, although he jumped every time she spoke to him. This house-hunting trip was a secret from Aunt Bella.

Tonio rowed the green gondola swiftly along the wide curves of the Grand Canal, whisking in and out among the other gondolas. Near the Rialto Bridge the canal was thick with boats: boats with orange sails full of silvery fish; boats piled high with green-and-gold melons; boats with big tubs of fresh water—sweet water Tonio called it—from the mainland; boats with cackling geese and chickens and ducks.

Uncle Maffeo swept a scornful thumb towards the big wooden bridge.

'Now in Cathay,' he bellowed, 'that bridge would be of stone: of fine carved stone; and it would be so wide that there would be shops along both sides. Kublai Khan wouldn't have such a rickety old bridge as that in the very meanest of his cities. This town needs waking up.'

'Be careful not to wake it up so that they begin throwing rotten peaches at you,' suggested Messer Nicolo. 'I see at least one face scowling at you already.'

Tonio saw the scowling face too—a fat, yellow face with a half-healed purple scar on the cheek. A scar that curved in almost the S-shaped way of the Grand Canal. Tonio did not think that Luigi Rosso was scowling because of Uncle Maffeo's ideas about bridges. Tonio worked hard at his oar and put as much distance as possible between him and Luigi.

Marco and Tonio had visited Luigi in the hospital and Marco had paid the doctor. Both boys had told Luigi they were sorry for what had happened, but the yellow-faced gondolier had not stopped scowling at Tonio whenever he saw him. He did not say that he meant to get even with him, but Tonio felt uneasy whenever he saw that scarred face. Somehow he was always seeing it.

He went so fast in trying to get out of Luigi's way this morning that he went too far down the Grand Canal.

'We've missed this canal with the long name,' said Messer Maffeo as Tonio shot through a clear space just under the Rialto Bridge. 'It's back farther. We want the Canal of San Giovanni Grisostomo. What a mouthful!'

Tonio turned the gondola. In a few moments they darted into the canal Messer Maffeo meant.

'How do you like that?' Maffeo Polo asked his brother, waving his hand towards a row of carved arches along the canal. 'Turn again to your right, Tonio, at the next corner. The entrance is from this other canal, the Rio San Marino.'

Tonio called 'Stalé' and swung the gondola around the sharp corner. They stopped at a flight of stone steps with green weed growing on the bottom step.

Building was still going on near-by. There were masses of shavings floating on the surface of the canal. The shavings were sprinkled with sawdust. Small triangles of new wood were caught in the thin curls. There was a smell of newly cut wood and the sound of saws and hammers.

Tonio followed the two brothers into a sunny courtyard. There was a clinking, chipping sound from an arched gateway on the north side of it. A man with a hammer and chisel was carving the stone of the arch, carving a bird such as neither

Tonio—nor probably anyone else—had ever seen. There was a pile of sand in the middle of the court. A man was mixing mortar in a wooden box.

'You see the house is almost finished,' said Messer Maffeo in a voice that echoed through the court and brought people to the windows of the houses on the other side. 'The man who was building it lost all his money. His fleet of ships, crammed with fine goods for England and Holland, was seized by pirates. He cannot pay the builders for the house and they must sell it to get their pay. Of course, they are asking too much for it, for like all builders they are the greediest rogues in the world— worse than pirates—but we might give them half what they ask. What do you say, Nicolo?'

Messer Maffeo grinned good-naturedly at the workmen, who grinned back. They did not seem to mind being called greedy rogues.

'Now I'll just show you over it,' Messer Maffeo went on. 'Don't say anything until you've seen it.'

Messer Nicolo had not said anything yet. He and Tonio followed Messer Maffeo quietly through the empty rooms.

'Now here, you see, Nicolo, we have room to store our goods,' roared Messer Maffeo. His voice echoed from the bare walls. 'All these rooms open on the canal with that name a yard long, San Giovanni Grisostomo. There are plenty of little rooms on this side where merchants can sleep when they come to trade with us. Then there's a quiet little place for a garden back of us. Nice for you, Nicolo. You like quiet, and the rest of the place is nice for me, for I like to be near the Grand Canal and the Rialto. And then Tonio can easily shoot me down to the Piazzetta so I can see what's going on, and stop in and tell the Doge how to improve the city. That wooden bridge now!

'And then on the next floor,' he went on, stumping up a carved staircase, 'there's a banquet hall that's big enough to swing an eel in, I can tell you. Not one of these little dark caves that you have to sit in with the children in your lap and everyone joggling your elbows just when you're going to swallow some spiced wine.'

Tonio thought the banquet hall was big enough to swing a dozen eels in if one could tie them together! It had a long row of arched windows looking out over the canal, and a wide, airy balcony.

'And there are plenty of rooms upstairs. Every Polo in Venice—cousins, uncles, aunts, brothers and sisters-in-law, and all the squalling children—can live here and have enough space. Well, Nicolo, what do you say?'

'I say yes,' said Messer Nicolo quietly. 'Only,' he added, with a twinkle in his blue-gray eyes, 'you'll have to break the news to Bella.'

Messer Maffeo groaned, but he did break the news to his sister. Madonna Bella hated any change. She protested in a voice that shook the plaster off the bricks—or at least so Messer Maffeo said—but in spite of her scolding the Polo family moved into the new house.

The carving of the archway, with its queer birds and beasts, its circles and flowers, was finished when Tonio saw it again. Above the arch was carved a cross, with circles at the ends of

it. To the left of that was a circle with a bird in it. If it was one of the Polos' starlings, it must be a very strong one, Tonio thought, as it seemed to be about to carry off an animal that was either a dog or a lamb: Tonio wasn't sure which.

The pile of sand was still in the middle of the court the day the Polos moved in. Playing in the sand was a little girl about four years old, with enormous blue-green eyes and hair that stuck out from under her cap like red-gold wire. She had on a dress almost the color of her eyes and stiff with gold embroidery: a dress that came down almost to her tiny feet in their little silk shoes. No one seemed to be looking after her.

She smiled at Marco Polo as he came through the arched gate after looking at the house, and threw a handful of sand at him.

Marco said good-naturedly: 'You mustn't throw sand, Madonna. It gets in people's eyes. Come, let's build a palace of it. Get us some water, Tonio.'

Tonio brought water from the well, and Marco built a castle out of the wet sand while the little girl patted cakes of it in her small pink hands.

'What's your name, Madonna?' asked Marco.

'Donata Loredano,' she said in a very clear voice. 'I know yours. You are Marco and you are going to live here always.'

'Am I?' asked Marco, smiling. 'I didn't know that.'

'Yes,' said Donata, with a nod of her copper-colored head. 'Your Aunt Bella told my mother so. I heard her. Quite loud. Is it time to kick the house down now?'

Marco said it was time and Donata kicked it down with her little blue shoes, which got rather damp.

'Now I will make something else,' said Marco. 'See, Tonio. You asked me where Cathay was. Now I will show you. See, I'll make Italy first. We think it's big, but it's smaller than one of Donata's slippers, and it's a little like one of Hans's boots. And here's Venice: up near the top of it on the right-hand side. And over here is Greece. Up above it is Constantinople, where my father

has big warehouses. Beyond that is a sea, a large one, and beyond that is another sea. And then, if you keep going long enough—going east, always east, every day towards the sunrise—you'll find Cathay.'

Tonio knelt down, looking at the marks in the sand.

'I wish I could go,' he said, 'and see the Great Khan and all those fine cities.'

Messer Maffeo's big voice boomed: 'You'll never get there with that map, boys. Why, you've made Italy as big as Persia! When you get out to Cathay, Italy doesn't look any bigger than a bean-pod, and Venice smaller than the smallest bean in it. Here, I'll show you.'

He rubbed out Marco's map and began again with his finger in the wet sand, murmuring names of strange towns and mountains and rivers. Marco and Tonio followed every motion of the stumpy finger, and listened to every word. Donata, however, soon lost interest in the road to Cathay, and wandered off.

'Now, here,' Messer Maffeo said, 'we can sell coral. The women wear all they can get. And it looks pretty enough on their dark skins. Down here at Hormuz we'll buy pearls: big smooth pearls with rainbows in them. It's hot there, so hot that people sit in the water up to their necks all day. No, they don't dive for pearls there: farther south. A man will splash in the water, they say, and stay under—What was that? Sounded like a splash.'

Marco jumped up from his knees. There was no sign of Donata's blue dress and coppery curls. He ran towards the canal and Tonio ran after him. Uncle Maffeo was not built for running. He followed more slowly. When Tonio reached the water, Marco's crimson cloak was on the stone landing place. Marco himself was in the water holding with one arm a very much soaked and frightened Donata and swimming with the other.

Donata's hair looked like brown seaweed instead of red-gold wire. Water and tears were streaming down her red cheeks. Her blue eyes were shut and her mouth was wide open. Choking sounds were coming out of it and now and then a howl. Tonio decided she was more frightened than hurt.

Marco handed her up to Tonio and came up the steps shaking the cold water out of his hair and ears. The tide was high and the water had the chill of autumn in it.

'Wring her out, Tonio,' he said. 'She weighs as much as a bag of wet salt. Why do you suppose women put all those clothes on a doll like that?'

'I'm not a doll,' sobbed Donata. 'I'm a big girl, catching fish for dinner.'

'Next time you want any fish, Donata, you ask me,' said Marco. 'I'll show you a better way to get them than swimming after them. Here, Tonio, give me my cloak.'

He wrapped the crimson cloak around Donata, who kicked a good deal, but finally threw both arms around Marco's neck and gave him a hug that almost choked him.

'I'm glad you have come to live in my courtyard,' said Donata.

Marco carried the wet bundle to the door of her own house and knocked at the door.

'I think it's lucky I'm going to live here, Madonna Donata,' he said, smiling at the damp but dignified child as he put her down. 'Someone will have to keep you in order.'

The hall of Donata's house was suddenly full of women who scolded the runaway and kissed her. Marco hurried off before anyone could thank him.

Tonio had found out already that Marco hated to be thanked.

CHAPTER 5

MOUNTAINS NEVER MEET

THE BIG palace on the Canal San Giovanni Grisostomo held all the Polo family comfortably just as Messer Maffeo had said it would. People began to call it the Ca' Polo—which was the Venetian way of saying the Polos' House. Something was always happening at the Ca' Polo. Boats kept stopping at the arched landing place and bringing goods to fill the big storerooms. Soft packs of wool came from England one day. Ostrich feathers from Egypt another. Fox and sable and ermine skins from Russia on a third. Sometimes the whole place would smell of cinnamon and allspice. On others there would be a fishy smell about it, and Tonio would know that Messer Maffeo would come upstairs with half a sturgeon's skin in his hand and offer his sister some of the salty, smoky eggs inside it.

'Caviar, my dear Bella. Have some. They're pearls, I tell you. Smoked pearls!' Messer Maffeo would shout.

Aunt Bella always refused with a scornful twitch of her long nose, and Messer Maffeo would grumble with his mouth full: 'You don't know what's good. Oh, well, all the more for me!'

And then he would always tell the same story about how some Russians he knew hid kegs full of caviar when they heard the Tartars were coming. The Russians buried the kegs and marked the place with three X's, and then built a fire on top to hide it.

'But the Tartars were too smart for them. They smelt it out with their flat noses. Ho! Ho!' Messer Maffeo would chuckle; 'but they didn't get this lot. Here, Tonio, clean out the skin. You know something good when you smell it, don't you?'

Tonio liked the queer fishy little eggs. In fact, he liked everything about the Ca' Polo. He liked red-haired Donata, who tagged after him and Marco wherever they went, and impish little Rosa Polo, who tagged after Donata. He liked cheerful, pink-faced young Maffeo, who was always getting into mischief and being dragged out of it by his older and more sensible brother. Tonio liked the meals in the big banquet hall, the talk of merchants from all over the world who were entertained by the Polo brothers. He liked the little room where Hans the German worked with gold and precious stones. Hans, Tonio discovered, was a wonderful craftsman. There was nothing he could not do with those long-fingered hands of his and the tiny hammers, files, and other tools that he always carried in his cowhide bag. It was the same bag that Tonio had heard clinking that bright morning at the Lido. Messer Maffeo had given it to Hans. The hair was wearing off the bag now. That morning seemed very long ago to Tonio.

Best of all Tonio liked the busy loading and unloading of boats. He always tried to be at the landing place when new cargoes came in. Before long he found he could help Marco keep track of them. Marco worked hard learning to read the different kinds of writing on bales and baskets. He and Tonio used to write down the things they learned about different kinds of goods—where they came from and how they were sold.

They would sit out on the arched gallery along the canal, hanging their feet over the singing water, and Marco would ask Tonio questions like this:

'Now, Tonio, at Constantinople what things are sold by the pound?'

Tonio would say, very fast, trying not to forget any: 'Wax, iron, tin, copper, pepper, ginger, cotton, cheese, oil, honey.'

'Very good. How much does it cost to take a camel load of silk from Tauris to Layos?'

'I've forgotten.'

'Bad. You ought to know. Two hundred and nine aspers. Does that include staying at the caravanserais? And the tolls on the bridges?'

'Yes.'

'Right. How is indigo sold?'

'In packages, about a hundred pounds in a package. You have to pay for the skin it's wrapped in. You can't unwrap it, but you can make a little hole and look in. Now let me ask one,' said Tonio. 'Suppose you buy a bag of rice—what about the rope?'

'You don't have to pay for the weight of the rope, but the seller keeps it,' said Marco.

The arched gallery was cool and shady one hot spring morning. The boys splashed their bare feet in the green water of the canal. Tonio was just explaining that if you bought almonds, you had to pay for the bag, but the buyer kept the bag, when a gentle voice, that Tonio recognized as Messer Nicolo's, said behind them: 'Why, We have a fine pair of merchants here. I believe you boys know more than I do! Tonio, is your gondola ready? I have to go to the Rialto.'

Both boys jumped up.

'Let me go too, father,' said Marco.

Messer Nicolo nodded, and the green gondola was soon skimming over the green water.

Tonio, swinging back and forward on the stern, looked very different from the skinny, rumpled boy Marco Polo had brought home more than a year before. The young gondolier's yellow curls were neatly cut now. They shone in the spring sunshine around a face that looked as if it never could have had hollow cheeks. The clothes that had been too big for him were now almost too small. His legs were sturdy, his arms strong, his shoulders broad.

Near the Rialto Bridge Messer Nicolo got out at a dark little shop in a crooked old house that looked as if it were almost ready to slide into the sparkling water. Tonio tied up the gondola to a dingy post with the paint peeling off it. Both boys followed Messer Nicolo into the shop.

It was very dark after the bright morning light. Tonio wondered what Messer Nicolo could possibly want in such a dull, dim place. Messer Nicolo had a leather bag with him, a heavy bag that chinked pleasantly as he swung into the shop and plunked it down on the counter.

A little brown-and-gray man as dingy as the shop lifted the bag with a skinny brown hand and smiled at Messer Nicolo showing sharp, white teeth. He had keen, brown eyes in a brown face, soft gray hair falling over his ears, and a thin gray beard. He wore a mouse-colored tunic, ragged brown stockings, and soft brown slippers in which he moved quickly, making little pattering noises.

'I am a poor man,' he announced, in a little squeaking voice, showing the sharp teeth. 'What can I do for you?'

'Show me a little of what makes you so poor,' said Messer Nicolo. 'A friend of mine is going on a journey. He wishes to change what is in this bag for something easily carried, Messer Giacomo.'

Messer Giacomo twisted about and suddenly produced a box. Out of it he began to take little packets wrapped in scraps of silk and velvet and pile them on the table in front of him. His thin brown fingers unwrapped the packets and Tonio began to see bright red and blue sparks and the yellow shine of gold. There were necklaces, rings and bracelets, strings of amber and coral. Except for the day Messer Maffeo had emptied Hans the German's bag, Tonio had never seen such beautiful things.

'If every lady at the Ca' Polo had three necks and ten arms she couldn't wear them all,' Tonio said to Marco.

'This is not Venetian work,' said Messer Nicolo, holding out a bracelet in the shape of a snake.

'Yet it was made right here in this very shop,' squeaked Messer Giacomo, pointing with a thin brown finger to a doorway behind Tonio.

All the time Tonio had been looking at the jewels he had heard the noise of someone working on metal at the back of the shop. There was a dusty brown curtain half-pulled across the door there. Tonio could see a man moving across the gap. He was a tall man, but he stood against the light and Tonio could not see his face. Something clanked and jingled when he moved.

The little jeweller squeaked out prices excitedly as he pushed rings and chains across to Messer Nicolo, and scratched down figures on a scrap of parchment. Messer Nicolo emptied his gold on the table and began to pile the silk and velvet-wrapped packets together.

'I shall need more,' he said. 'You had better bring them to my house.'

Messer Giacomo squeaked: 'I am proud to do business with Messer Nicolo Polo.'

There was a queer noise from behind the curtain, a gasp followed by a crash and a loud jangling of metal.

The brown curtain was shoved aside and a man stood in the opening, holding out his hands to Messer Nicolo and speaking very fast in words Tonio did not understand. He was a tall man with a pale, thin face, for which his dark eyes seemed too big. They looked sad and so did his mouth. He had an ugly nose, Tonio thought, large and hooked, but somehow Tonio liked his face. He was poorly dressed. Everything about him was ragged except his leather apron.

He pulled a moth-eaten old fur cap off his crisp black curls as he spoke to Messer Nicolo, but he did not move beyond the doorway. There was soot on his arms and little bright specks of gold filings on his pale skin.

'Mar Sarghis!' exclaimed Messer Nicolo. 'How did you get here?'

The man began to speak in the Venetian way, but slowly and haltingly.

'When I left you at Aleppo,' he said, 'I went back towards Tauris, guiding another party of merchants. Barka Khan's Tartars—may every one of them be buried with one of his own arrows through his flat face!—robbed us. They killed some of us. The rest they sold as slaves. Because I had some skill with metal, I was sold instead of killed. This is the kind of stirrup I wear now, Messer Nicolo.'

He moved his foot a little.

There was an iron ring around his ankle and a chain that ran back into the room behind him.

Messer Nicolo turned to the jeweller.

'I believe I have bought the wrong kind of jewel,' he said. He pushed the packets back across the table. 'Another day, Messer Giacomo, will do for these, but today I must ask a favor of you. This man was my guide across deserts and mountains. Places so far off that you would only laugh if I told you how far. And once he saved my life. No matter how, but when I said good-bye, I thanked him, and said that I was glad that we parted as friends, for, as the saying is, "Mountains never meet—but men do." Perhaps we should meet again, I said, in spite of all the land and water between us. So now that we have met, Messer Giacomo, I think it will be a good time for me to pay my debt to him. Show me the paper that tells what you paid for him and take twice whatever it was out of that pile of ducats. You can bring the jewels another day.'

Tonio heard Mar Sarghis give a kind of sob, saw the little jeweller unfasten the chains and fetters with a key almost as long as his brown hand, saw a stream of gold ducats drop into the box with the packets of jewels.

Mar Sarghis looked very white as he came out into the sunshine. It was too bright for his dark eyes and he shut them for a moment, then limped down the steps to the gondola. He hardly spoke as they went back to the Ca' Polo, but only looked about him as if he were in a strange world.

Once he said: 'My city of Tyre was beautiful once, before you destroyed it.'

Messer Nicolo said gently: 'Don't say I destroyed it, Mar Sarghis. You know that merchants don't like wars. They would rather trade with a city than burn it.' Then he added with a smile: 'And didn't a certain Mar Sarghis, and a German fellow with hair like straw, make some great machines for Kublai Khan so that he could throw rocks into a city he wanted? What kind of work do you suppose your machines—we call them mangonels, Tonio—are doing now in Cathay, Mar Sarghis?'

The big Tyrian looked more cheerful.

'That was a fine mangonel!' he said. 'How the walls fell when the rocks hit them! The noise was like a whole mountain falling. A pity we couldn't see the end of it.'

'Should you like to go back to Cathay?' asked Messer Nicolo.

'Tomorrow!' exclaimed Mar Sarghis. 'When do we start?'

Tonio wished Messer Nicolo would answer the question, but the merchant only smiled.

'I'd like to see Hans again,' said Mar Sarghis.

'Why, you can do that,' Messer Nicolo said, 'without going farther than the next canal.'

Tonio swung the gondola around the corner and there was Hans at the door of the warehouse of the Ca' Polo. His pale blue eyes grew round with surprise when he saw Mar Sarghis. He opened his mouth wide and began to talk very fast, first in German, then in the Tartar language, with a few words of Persian and the Venetian tongue put in here and there.

One word that Tonio kept hearing was Sayanfu. It puzzled him and Marco too. Marco asked his father what it meant.

'It's the name of a city in Cathay,' said Messer Nicolo. 'Kublai Khan tried to capture it, but there was a great lake at the back of it so the people could always get plenty of food. They were little yellow men with slant eyes—Chinese. No good as fighters, but the Tartars could not break through the strong walls of the city to fight. And they could not starve them out because of the lake. Boats came across it every day with food. The Khan was angry. The Chinese were making a fool of him. One day Maffeo said to him: "We'll take Sayanfu for you, Sir Emperor. My brother and I have two followers who can make machines that will grind those walls to powder." So Hans and Mar Sarghis built a mangonel that would throw great rocks against the walls. We had to go on our errand to the Pope before the walls fell, but Mar Sarghis heard in Persia that the city was taken by the Khan not long after we left Cathay. So now these two goldsmiths are fighting the whole battle over just as if they'd been there.'

'They're dangerous fellows by the sound,' said Marco, laughing.

'A man who can make a gold necklace one day and shoot down a stone tower the next is quite useful,' said Messer Nicolo. 'As you'll find when—I mean if—you ever go to Cathay.'

THE MERCHANT'S RHYME

MARCO POLO said to Tonio: 'Do you notice anything different lately, Tonio?'

Tonio nodded his yellow head gravely. There had been a great deal to notice since the day Mar Sarghis was found. The big storerooms of the Ca' Polo were filled to the ceilings with goods. Messer Giacomo pattered in and out. Other jewellers, too, came with small bundles and left with pouches of gold and silver. A man from one of the glass furnaces brought bags of beads that looked almost like jewels. Hans and Mar Sarghis were busy stringing them and making clasps for them. In the room where the Big Tyrian and the little German worked, Tonio often saw Messer Nicolo and Messer Maffeo sitting at a table with heaps of flashing stones before them, sorting them, making lists of them, tying them into small packages wrapped in soft leather.

He and Marco helped to pack the strings of beads and to make lists of them; and lists, too, of small ornaments of mosaic—pictures of birds and animals and flowers all made of tiny pieces of glass cleverly fitted together.

One morning Messer Maffeo called Marco and Tonio into the jewel room.

'Which of you boys can recite the "Rhyme of the Merchant"?' he asked.

'I can!' said both boys together.

'Say it then. Take turns. Begin, Marco.'

Marco Polo looked straight at his uncle with his clear gray eyes and began:

> *'Honesty is always best.*
> *Always look before you leap.*
> *Make no easy promises*
> *That you do not mean to keep.*
> *Courtesy is never lost.*
> *Civil words pay all they cost.'*

Messer Maffeo smiled and nodded to Tonio, who went on with the next verse:

> *'"Cheap to buy and dear to sell"*
> *Merchants say is wisdom clearest.*
> *Older heads have learned as well,*
> *"Cheapest goods may prove the dearest."*
> *Go to church and always spare*
> *Him who sends thy gains a share.'*

Then both boys said together:

> *'You'll prosper standing by one price,*
> *And shunning fighting, drinking, dice.*
> *Take heed to govern well thy pen*
> *And blunder not in black and white. Amen.'*

Both voices came to the last word with such force that the little room rang with it.

Maffeo Polo turned to his brother with a pleased air. 'I told you so,' he said.

Messer Nicolo smiled his kind smile.

'You didn't have to prove it to me, Maffeo,' he said. 'I knew you were right.'

He looked at the boys a minute, still smiling, and then said softly: 'Who wants to go to Cathay? Any young merchants here?'

Marco Polo sprang forward.

'Do you mean it, father?' he said. 'Are you really going to take me?'

'I'll need you,' said Messer Nicolo.

Tonio had not said anything. He did not think that Messer Nicolo could really mean that he was to go to Cathay too, but in a moment Marco's father added: 'And Tonio, too.'

Marco said suddenly: 'Who's going to tell Aunt Bella?' His uncle grinned and said: 'Why, you may tell her, Marco. That shall be your first duty.'

'I'd rather stay at home,' said Marco, laughing.

'Ho!' said Uncle Maffeo. 'Afraid of a woman! Well, I sup—pose I shall have to tell her myself. I always have to do all the hard jobs. Luckily I have courage.'

Just then they were called to dinner. Towards the end of the meal, Uncle Maffeo had a good chance to show his courage.

Aunt Bella turned suddenly to her brother Maffeo and said in her shrill voice:

'Maffeo Polo, it is time you shaved off that beard of yours. It isn't fashionable to wear any such bush on your chin. You look like a fat crow sticking his head out of his nest.'

The brave Messer Maffeo looked nervously, first at his sister, then at his brother.

'These are delicious ripe figs, my dear Bella,' he said. 'Where do you get them?'

Aunt Bella paid no attention to this remark, but turned to Messer Nicolo.

'And you, Nicolo,' she said, 'look like a ragged brown bear. None of our Venetians wear these mats of hair.'

Messer Nicolo said quietly: 'But when we merchants have to travel among the Tartars, we always wear beards. You see the Tartars haven't any beards to speak of—a few scraggly hairs, perhaps, like black bristles that they like to call beards, that's all. So they rather admire ours.'

'That might be all very well if you were going to travel among the Tartars,' snapped Madonna Bella, 'but as you're not—'

'But you see, my dear Bella, we are,' said Messer Nicolo, smiling gently at his sister.

Of course, Aunt Bella did all the things that her brothers were afraid she would do. She shrieked and cried and scolded.

'That's right!' she sobbed. 'Go off again for nine more years and leave me all alone, just the way you did before, to look after your children!'

'We're taking Marco with us,' said Messer Nicolo. 'You'll have only young Maffeo to look after this time.'

But Aunt Bella only sobbed louder.

'Marco going! My favorite nephew!' she said. 'The only one who ever has a kind word for his old aunt! I shall die of loneliness! And, of course, he'll be killed by those Tartars. Or he'll marry a Tartar. He'll bring one home here to murder us all in our beds.'

Messer Nicolo pointed out that after all, with twelve or fifteen other members of the family living at the Ca' Polo, Aunt Bella would not be exactly alone. Marco promised that he would not marry a Tartar girl, but Aunt Bella still sobbed.

'Besides,' said Messer Nicolo, 'we shall not be gone long this time. We shall escort the Pope's messengers and then travel straight home again.'

'And it will only take you seven years!' sniffed Aunt Bella. 'You don't call seven years anything, I suppose! Why, Marco will be a man by then—with one of those awful beards probably.'

Tonio looked at Marco and smiled. He wondered how Marco would look with a beard.

'Perhaps,' he thought, 'I'll have a beard too. I do hope it won't make me look like a field after the corn is cut—like Hans.'

Marco made a sign to Tonio and the two boys slipped out into the courtyard, where out of pure joy they began to tumble each other around and punch each other.

'We're going to Cathay!' said Marco, grabbing Tonio around the waist and trying to throw him down.

'To see Kublai Khan!' shouted Tonio, butting Marco in the ribs with his yellow head.

'We'll ride on camels!' gasped Marco, getting one arm around Tonio's neck and choking him.

'And elephants!' sputtered Tonio, twisting one of his legs in its black stocking between Marco's red ones.

Marco rolled over and came up smiling.

'I'll shoot one of those red and black-and-white-striped lions,' he boasted.

'No, I will,' said Tonio, sitting on Marco's stomach.

He felt someone pushing him and looked over his shoulder. Donata was standing behind him thumping his back with her small fists.

'Don't hurt my Marco,' she said, scowling at Tonio.

Tonio laughed and let Marco get up.

'You're a bad boy, Tonio Tumba,' Donata said, shaking her red curls. 'I wish you'd go away.'

'I'm going,' said Tonio meekly. 'A long way off, to Cathay.'

'Good,' said Donata. 'Then I'll play with Marco.'

'Marco's going too,' Tonio remarked.

Donata did not scream and cry like Aunt Bella, but her blue-green eyes seemed to grow even bigger as she looked at Marco. At last two tears trickled out of them and ran down her short, freckled nose. They were two of the largest tears Tonio had ever seen.

'Don't cry, Donata,' he said hastily. 'I'll bring you something from Cathay.'

'So will I,' said Marco. 'What should you like?'

Donata rubbed the tears away with the back of her hand. 'A kitten. No, a puppy. No, both,' she said.

'I'll bring you one, and Tonio the other,' Marco promised. 'Don't forget me, will you, Donata?'

Donata looked up at him. Her sea-blue eyes were still a little damp, but she smiled and shook her coppery head in its little cap of velvet and pearls.

'I won't forget you, Marco Polo,' she said clearly. 'Not ever. Especially not if you bring the puppy.'

The next few days went so quickly that Tonio hardly knew which end he was standing on. A big fleet of trading galleys was being made ready to start for ports at the eastern end of the Mediterranean. Down at the arsenal a new galley was being finished for the Polos. There was a great ringing of hammers all day and all night and a strong smell of hot pitch. The old

galleys were being painted with all sorts of gay colors, fitted out with new oars, new coils of rope, new sails; men were painting the sails, dipping sponges into pans of red and orange and blue, dabbing the white canvas with the sponges, and soaking the sails in salt water to set the colors. Tonio saw a man paint a very cross-looking lion of San Marco, and a shield with three ragged blackbirds on a sail for the Polos' new ship. The man let Tonio sponge on some of the blue behind the lion's head, and let Marco put red on the Polo shield. Tonio felt proud of his painting.

He was not at all pleased when Rosa pointed out that he had put a good deal of blue on the lion's ears, and even more on his own chin.

Rosa, of course, was looking on. The whole Polo family had gone down to the shipyard to see the new galley. Tonio wished they had left Rosa at home.

'Tonio thinks he's wonderful,' she told everyone loudly. 'He ought not to go to Cathay. He ought to stay at home and paint lions with blue ears.'

Marco picked up a sponge and said: 'I'll paint your ears blue if you don't look out. You little bumble-bee.'

'If you get paint on my new dress, I'll tell Aunt Bella.'

Rosa danced around the two boys and stuck out a very pointed red tongue.

> '*Messer Tonio Tumblekin*
> *Got a sponge to paint his chin,*'
she sang, still dancing.

'Don't pay any attention to her, Tonio,' said Marco. 'She's only a baby.'

'I am not a baby. I'm nine years old.

> '*Tonio Tumba and Marco too*
> *Painted their faces red and blue,*'
sang Rosa.

There really wasn't any red paint on Marco's chin, but he put his hand up to it and got both red and blue paint on it. Of course this delighted Rosa. She sang her song all over again several times, dodging behind the groups of sail painters. This time it was Tonio who advised Marco not to pay any attention to her. Marco was chasing her, promising to stuff the sponge in her mouth.

'Let her sing,' said Tonio. 'What do we care, anyway? We'll soon be starting for Cathay.'

It seemed as if the day would never come to load the galley, but it did come at last. Tonio and Marco worked as hard as any of the porters, making lists of bales and boxes and hampers and bags. It seemed as if the galley could never hold them all. There were boxes of soap, jars of olive oil from Spain, bales of wool and of fine scarlet cloth from England, sacks of broken coral, bundles of brocades and velvets from Venice, wine from France and linen from Holland. When everything was packed, the cargo was covered with ox-hides so that no water could spoil it.

Marco and Tonio hardly slept at all the night before the fleet sailed. Tonio was quite sure that he had never shut his eyes at all, but he had a hard time opening them when Marco began pulling him by one foot just before dawn.

Marco looked very tall in the dim light. The moon was just going down and shone faintly into Tonio's room. Tonio got up shivering and dressed hurriedly in the new suit of heavy blue cloth that Messer Nicolo had given him. His gondolier's clothes hung on the wall, looking very limp and empty. A new boy was going to wear them that very day. Tonio wondered if Rosa Polo would pinch the new gondolier at dinner time. She and Tonio had not parted in a very friendly way. Rosa had put sand down his neck the day before and Tonio had chased her with a dead eel. The eel had got sandy too somehow. The cook was planning to put it into a fish stew for dinner and Tonio had been well scolded. Rosa had laughed at him, made faces and called 'Tonio Tumba' in a teasing voice, and joggled his elbow when he was passing his last bowl of gravy.

'Altogether too fresh' was what Tonio thought about Rosa.

The two boys slipped down through the silent house, got into the green gondola for the last time. Tonio made it skim through the twisting canal and over the dark water to the Piazzetta. The light in the bell tower was still burning. The shadows of the tall granite columns and the figures at their tops were dark on the pavement. Marco and Tonio ran across the Piazzetta and in to the larger square in front of the Church of San Marco. It was very quiet there. The palaces around it were all dark. The pigeons were asleep among the domes and turrets. The moonlight and the flickering light from the bell tower shone on the backs of the bronze horses above the porch of the church. They looked dark against the pale sky as the boys hurried under them. In the church there was a sort of golden twilight. Candles around the altar made a bright haze through which the boys could see here and there the shine of gold and jewels among the shadows. There was a sweet, spicy smell of incense and burning wax.

Both boys knelt down before the altar. The gold screen behind it glowed with jewels. The rubies were like hot coals of fire. When they got up from their knees, Marco whispered to Tonio, 'I have promised San Marco to bring back some rubies as fine as any of these.'

Tonio had not thought of anything so grand.

'I will bring something to San Marco's Church too,' he said as they went out. 'Because everyone must. He takes care of the city. But I must bring the same or better to the Church of San Nicolo at the Lido, because he took care of me when I was poor and brought me to your house, Marco. Only I don't know what to bring.'

'Well,' said Marco practically, 'perhaps it would be better to decide that when you see what you get.'

Tonio thought Marco was probably right, but he noticed that Marco had no doubt about finding plenty of rubies. But then, of course, Marco was different. He always knew what he wanted to do and always found some way to do it. Tonio wished he could be more like him.

It was getting light when they came out of the church. The dawn was making the palaces look like the inside of a shell—all faint pink and blue.

The green gondola slid along towards the Lido with the tide.

'We are early,' said Tonio. 'I should like to stop at San Nicolo's Church. I have brought two fat candles to light for him.'

There were other gondolas following them. As Tonio tied the green gondola to the painted post at the landing near the church, a black gondola stopped beside him. Tonio saw the yellow face of Luigi Rosso. The curved scar on the man's fat cheek was still purple. It turned a darker reddish color as he saw Tonio and Marco.

Tonio got out of the gondola.

'Don't stay too long, Tonio,' Marco called after him. 'You know I'm going to Cathay.'

Luigi Rosso said in a voice as smooth as olive oil running out of a bottle:

'Let us part friends, Messer Marco, since you are going on such a long journey. Let me take you across the harbor. I have not forgotten how you paid the doctors for me. To take you to the dock in my gondola would be only a small payment, I know, but I should be honored if you would accept such a worthless favor.'

Marco called after Tonio again.

'Tonio! Luigi's going to row me across. Come along when you're ready.'

Tonio said, 'All right, Marco,' and stepped into the dark church.

He lighted his two big candles and watched the face of the kind old Saint smile at him in their twinkling light. Tonio had not thought what San Nicolo would like from Cathay, but he felt sure he would find something wonderful.

Tonio stayed longer than he meant to in the quiet church. As he came out into the hot sunshine, a galley full of singing people went past him. Tonio hurried towards the post to which he had tied his gondola. He knew the post by its freshly painted blue-and-orange stripes. They shone cheerfully in the sunlight—but the green gondola was gone!

The galley had gone too. The sheet of water in front of him was empty. All the boats in Venice seemed to be tangled in a bright-colored mass on the other side of it. The only things that broke the rippling water were big weed-covered rocks. They were thrusting themselves slowly higher as the breeze from the north and the tide pushed and pulled the dancing water towards the Lido.

Tonio said, half aloud: 'The tide. It's going. The ships will go with it.'

His voice choked and he could hardly breathe.

'I know I tied the rope tight. I know I did!' he said, almost sobbing. 'Oh, they'll go! They'll go without me! Everyone's gone. My gondola, my gondola! Who would take it?'

The answer flashed into his mind as he asked himself the question. He knew well enough who would like to do him a bad turn!

'Luigi Rosso shan't stop me!' said Tonio fiercely. 'A gondola isn't the only fish that can swim in this water.'

The water looked cold. The north wind had already set Tonio's teeth chattering. He stood shivering on the bank to see if a boat might be coming. The lagoon was sparkling and empty. He looked towards the masts of the distant galleys. They were setting their sails. Suddenly behind one of the weed-covered rocks something moved and the sun flashed on the beak of a gondola. The tide pushed it along a little. It was painted green.

Tonio threw himself, clothes and all, into the water. He

swam fast—faster than he ever had before—but the gondola seemed as far away as ever. The tide had pulled it into the main channel and it bobbed along now like a curled-up leaf in a hurrying brook.

Tonio's clothes were getting heavier and heavier. His arms ached, but he swam on, panting and ducking through the ripples like a young dolphin. His side hurt. It grew harder and harder to breathe. He opened his mouth for air. A wave slapped against his face. It choked him, but he plunged on.

The gondola went on too, gaily, lightly, always a little ahead. At last, just as Tonio felt that he could not move his arms much longer, it bumped against another rock and stopped, caught for a moment by the green-and-brown weed.

The weed held it just long enough. The rope was trailing in the water. Tonio grabbed it, a puff of wind caught the gondola and it started to move again, but Tonio's hands were on the side. He pulled himself over the edge and lay for a moment in the bottom of the boat gasping, dripping, shivering. His cold, blue fingers still clutched the rope tightly. There was something queer about the rope. The knot he had tied in it to keep it from fraying was gone. The rope had been cut cleanly above the knot. The cut ends still looked new. Tonio thought he knew whose knife had made that cut.

Luckily the gondola oar was in its place. Tonio stood up and began to work it. The north wind seemed to blow right through his thick clothes. He felt wetter than ever. The distance to the dock and the fleet of shining galleys was short, now that he had his boat again, but before he reached the dock the galleys had begun to leave.

Tonio's arms had never felt so weak. Every tug at his oar seemed like the last motion he could make.

'They'll go!' he thought. 'I shall never see Cathay. Aunt Bella won't want me when Marco is gone. The new boy has my clothes already. I shall be on the canals again. Cold. Hungry. Lonely. Luigi will laugh at me. Beat me. Smash my boat.'

His side began to ache again. He could hardly breathe, but somehow he kept on.

The noise of the departing fleet began to ring in his ears. He heard trumpets and the roll of drums. People were singing and talking and laughing. The sun shone on bright dresses and on polished shields and swords.

The landing on Tonio's side of the dock was full of empty gondolas. He shoved his in among them. There was a burst of music and shouting.

'Another galley gone!' he thought. 'They've forgotten me!'

He ran along the dock with feet that slipped, with water dripping and spattering from his soaking clothes.

He dashed around a corner and ran against a solidly built boy travelling almost as fast as he was. It was Marco.

'I was just going for you,' he said. 'I was afraid something had happened to you. Why, Tonio, you're all wet! Stop and get your breath. We've still a few minutes before the galley goes. What's the matter?'

'That Luigi,' panted Tonio, 'cut my rope. I had to swim.'
Marco scowled.

'Are you sure? I don't see what he'd do that for.'

'I don't either,' Tonio gasped. 'I should think he'd want to get rid of me. Not keep me in Venice.'

Marco said: 'Oh, but I see now. He thought you were going to stay. He said to me something about your owning the Ca' Polo while I was in Cathay. But I just told him to keep his ideas to himself. If I could get hold of the fat rogue now—but he's gone. He went back to the city when he left me.'

'Oh, well,' said Tonio—he could breathe better now—'we've seen the last of his fat face for a while.'

'Yes,' said Marco, 'and if he keeps on doing tricks like that, he'll be hanged long before we get back to Venice.'

'I hope you're right about that,' said Tonio.

Chapter 7

GOOD-BYE, VENICE!

'Stand here in the sun,' said Marco, 'and get dry.'

Tonio leaned against a hot stone wall and watched the crowd. All Venice, it seemed, had come to see the galleys slide out from the silver of the lagoon and whisk over the bright water of the Adriatic, with the crisp north wind filling the freshly painted sails. The Doge was there with a robe of gold and ermine over his dress of scarlet velvet and silver brocade. The sun winked on the jewels of his cap with the horn at the back, on the gold umbrella that a boy in silver and scarlet tried to hold over his head. The boy was very short and the Doge very tall. The boy's fat arms got so stiff trying to hold up the umbrella, and his fat legs got so tired trotting after the Doge's long thin ones, his round face so hot and red, that Tonio felt sorry for him.

'Pretty hard luck,' Tonio thought, 'to have to stay in Venice all your life and chase a tall man with an umbrella.'

Two more boys dressed like the other carried the Doge's

stool and a cloth-of-gold cushion. They had to travel fast to keep up with him, and were just as useless as the umbrella boy, because the Doge never sat down. There were men tooting on silver trumpets and clanging silver cymbals who marched after the Doge and tried hard not to trip over the boys. The Doge's sword-bearer was there, too, with a wonderful sword in a sheath of silver and gold with jewels in the hilt.

The Admiral of the fleet, in his violet and crimson silks, walked with the Doge and cheered the different galleys as they flew past. The Doge's silver trumpets all sounded for each galley and the trumpets and drums on the galleys answered. The crossbowmen and sailors shouted. The gentlemen of Venice, in their short black cloaks, their embroidered tunics and bright hose, waved their gay caps and cheered the flying boats.

Tonio slipped on board without going near Aunt Bella. He did not want her to see that his fine new clothes were already stained with the salty water of the lagoon. He was afraid that if Aunt Bella found out that he had been in the water that morning, she would somehow succeed in keeping him from going to Cathay. He thought it would be safer to say good-bye after he was on the galley.

Besides, Tonio did not want to say good-bye. He wanted to go to Cathay, of course, more than anything in the world. And he had planned a nice little speech to Aunt Bella, thanking her for being so good to him. Because she had been good to him, even if she did like to scold. She nipped people, Tonio thought, the way crabs claw, but she was good inside like a crab's claw.

He had not planned to tell her that. His speech was going to be very dignified and polite. Only somehow he could not make it. It made him feel queer inside when he thought about it, so he squeezed behind Marco and looked over his shoulder, and smiled and waved until his arm was stiff in his wet sleeve.

The silver trumpets sounded their loudest as the Polos' galley, with its bright flag and streamers and the three black birds on the sail, cut into the rough water of the sea. Tonio saw all the gay crowd—the Doge in his splendid robes, all the gold and silver and rich color—but the thing that he remembered the most clearly was the group from the Ca' Polo. Aunt Bella, in her best and brightest purple dress, with tears trickling down her long nose, waved a skinny hand. Young Maffeo tried hard to keep his pink face cheerful, but there was a funny twist about his mouth. All the rest of the Polo family—the aunts, the uncles, the cousins, the brothers and sisters-in-law, even a new gondolier, already wearing Tonio's outgrown clothes—waved and shouted. Rosa made a face at Tonio. She had her hands behind her back. Suddenly she brought the right one forward and threw something towards the galley. It splashed into the water near the dock. It was a very dead eel!

Tonio stuck out his tongue and yelled, 'Good shot!' but there was so much noise that he was afraid Rosa did not hear.

Everyone was calling to them: 'Good-bye, Nicolo! Goodbye, Maffeo! Good-bye, Marco! Tell us all about it, Marco, when you get home! Be sure you learn some good stories! Good-bye, Tonio! Marco, bring me home a string of pearls! Good-bye, Hans! Don't try to spend paper money in Constantinople! Uncle Maffeo, bring me some gold silk from Yezd! Good-bye, Mar Sarghis! You'll soon be on a camel again. Don't fall off! Don't let Tonio fall off! Uncle Nicolo, I want a sword with three blades. Don't forget! From Damascus. Good-bye! Good-bye! Come back soon!'

The last words Tonio heard were Donata's.

'I won't forget you, Marco! Bring me my puppy! Tonio, don't forget my little cat!'

The voices grew fainter. The figures grew smaller and smaller. Soon they were only bright splashes of color. Rosa's crimson dress was only as big as a rose leaf; Donata's no bigger than a violet. Before long Venice itself, master of the Adriatic, had sunk down below those twinkling, foaming, slapping waves. The gold roof of the bell tower was like a bright star, but at last it disappeared too. The waves were big and green. One, even bigger than the others, pitched the stern of the galley high into the air. Tonio had one last glimpse of the shining tower.

Tonio felt very queer. He was not quite sure whether he was homesick or seasick. In a few minutes he knew that he was both!

Before the long journey to Acre was over, Tonio was as good a sailor as anyone.

'You're in good training for the Ship of the Desert,' bellowed Uncle Maffeo, slapping Tonio between his shoulders and almost knocking him overboard.

Tonio looked eagerly at the shore. He thought he would see long caravans of camels right away, but there were none anywhere, only rocks and trees and mountains. Before long they were within sight of Acre with all its high walls and towers.

Marco said: 'This is the finest city in the world—except one!'

Uncle Maffeo roared with laughter. 'A duckling hatched out one morning. "This is the biggest ocean I ever saw," he said, looking at the duck pond—"except my mother's drinking-dish!"'

Tonio liked the walled city, too, but both boys grew very tired of it before they left it. There were many delays before they finally started with the Pope's letters and the oil from the lamp at the Holy Sepulchre in Jerusalem. Kublai Khan had asked for that oil. He had asked, too, for a hundred priests and wise men to

teach his people. The Polos got the oil from the holy lamp, but the Pope could send only two priests instead of the hundred for whom Kublai Khan had asked, and these two priests, greatly to the disgust of the Polos, became frightened almost before the journey to Cathay had begun and went back to Acre. They were afraid of being killed by the Tartars, they said. They had heard that there was fighting among the Tartar tribes.

'Of course there is,' said Messer Maffeo disgustedly. 'Tartars fight all the time. It's their business. And their exercise. But they won't hurt ambassadors to the Great Khan, properly guarded. Come along now. I myself will take care of you.'

Messer Maffeo thumped his big chest and puffed out his fat red cheeks above his curly black beard, but the priests went back just the same. The Polos went on, taking the letters of the Pope with them.

At first Tonio could not get used to the slowness of that journey. He had thought that he and Marco would ride swiftly every day on camels or fine horses, with Messer Maffeo and Messer Nicolo ahead, flashing those tablets of gold as they went. But instead of prancing gaily across Asia, most of the time, Tonio found, was spent in waiting.

Even with the gold tablets and the Pope's letters, the Polos' little party could not travel safely alone. The Tartars, as Messer Maffeo explained cheerfully, would kill you first and look at the tablets afterward. So the three Polos, Hans the German, Mar Sarghis, and Tonio had to wait until they could travel with parties of sixty or a hundred people. It took a long time for enough people to gather, and when they had at last agreed to set off, it seemed to take an endless time for them to get started. Packing goods into oxcarts, tying bales on camels, saddling horses and asses, all were done as if the day were forty-eight hours long.

Tonio and Marco soon found out that a caravan moves only as fast as the slowest beast in it.

'We could walk to Cathay as fast as we're going,' Tonio said to Marco.

'Yes,' Marco agreed, 'but if we went too fast, we might miss seeing something.'

Marco never missed seeing anything. He visited the market places and talked to the shopkeepers. Mar Sarghis could speak half a dozen different tongues and Marco learned to speak them all, and how to write some of them. He found out about the things that were made in whatever town he was in. He noticed the things that grew in the country around. He learned about the different animals of the country. He peered into churches that sometimes were like those in Venice, but that grew less and less like them as he travelled farther east. He learned about

the different kinds of money the people used—gold and silver and copper coins, little wedges of metal, white shells that were called 'porcellami'—which means little pigs—and sometimes cakes of salt.

'And when we get to Cathay,' said Hans the German, pulling a piece of yellow paper out of his pouch, 'we'll spend this.'

It was the very yellow paper with the red seal, much crumpled from being so long in the German's pouch, that Hans had offered Tonio that morning in Venice.

'Shall we ever get there, do you think, Hans?' asked Tonio. 'Why, we haven't even seen any Tartars yet. I don't believe there are any. Marco makes up the stories about them that he pretends to hear in the market places.'

'I do, do I?' growled Marco, riding up beside Tonio and putting a finger in a spot between two ribs—a spot that tickled and made Tonio laugh and gasp.

'Stories about mountains that move and eagles that go into valleys and bring up diamonds in hunks of raw meat. Wonderful stories!' Tonio gasped.

'Yes. Very good stories,' Marco agreed. 'People like to hear them.'

'They've liked to hear them a long time,' chuckled Mar Sarghis. 'They're just as good as ever. Only a thousand years old or so. How well they've worn!'

Marco only smiled good-naturedly.

'Some people,' he said, 'can't believe things even when they see them.'

He looked out across the rolling grassy plain over which they were travelling. The caravan was strung out behind them following a narrow, dusty track that curved like a snake through the waving grass. Marco glanced back at it for a moment, then turned his keen gray eyes again towards the northeast.

'What should you say,' he asked carelessly, 'if I told you I saw a city moving?'

'That you were crazy,' answered Tonio promptly. 'Cities don't move.'

'What do you say, Mar Sarghis?' asked Marco. He raised his scarlet leather whip and pointed out across the plain. 'Shall we wait and let the caravan catch up with us?'

The tall Tyrian narrowed his black eyes until they were only slits in his sunburned face.

'Halt!' he said, with his hand on Tonio's bridle rein. 'You are right, Messer Marco.'

Suddenly Tonio saw what Marco had seen. A small stream wound along a fold in the plain. Along the other side of it, half-hidden by the scrubby willows and bushes that grew along its bank, something was moving. The sun shone on white things like the domes of a city. Only these domes were close to the ground, and moving slowly, steadily, along the green banks of the brown river. They had been hidden behind a rolling grassy hill. More and more kept coming out from behind it.

'They're like beehives,' said Tonio. 'Hundreds of beehives.'

And there are bees in them that sting,' said Mar Sarghis. 'You'll see some Tartars, Tonio, before you're much older.'

CHAPTER 8

TARTARS

THE REST of the caravan hurried towards the place where Marco and Tonio were waiting. Tonio heard Messer Maffeo shouting: 'Get behind the carts! Take out the oxen! Make a square! Animals inside! Men, kneel down behind your packs!'

Everyone moved quickly now. Bales and packs were hastily piled in a square. Men unsheathed their swords and strung their bows. Tonio was sent into the middle of the square to hold the horses. He wished he could have stayed beside Marco. He saw Marco kneeling behind a bale of silk with his bow beside him, smoothing the feathers of his arrows. He was whistling cheerfully and looking with his far-sighted, shining eyes at the moving white domes.

Beyond the domes horsemen were galloping over the grass. They wheeled suddenly and dipped down towards the river. Tonio could see them splashing through the shallow water.

The legs of their shaggy horses shone wet as they galloped uphill towards the caravan.

'Don't shoot,' said Messer Nicolo, in his clear, calm voice. 'They may be friendly.'

'No good Tartars but dead Tartars!' muttered Mar Sarghis, twanging his bowstring.

The Tartars were near the square now. Tonio could see their iron helmets, their leather-covered shields, and their faces as flat as the shields and almost of the same color. He could hear the soft thudding of the horses' feet and in the dust smell the harsh odor of sweating horses. The men shouted as they rode. They sounded, Tonio thought, like a pack of dogs yelping and growling. It made a queer feeling run down his backbone.

He saw Messer Nicolo standing on top of a wooden box. Tonio remembered that there were crystal goblets carefully packed in it—a present from the Pope to Kublai Khan. He hoped they would not be broken, and then felt angry with himself for worrying about the crystal goblets when Messer Nicolo himself was in danger.

The tall merchant stood quietly with his eyes fixed on the thundering mass of horsemen. Tonio saw him raise the Khan's golden tablet above his head. The sharp little eyes of the Tartars must have seen it flash, for they checked their horses a bowshot from the caravan. Dust puffed up under the horses' feet. The Tartars stopped their yelping and stood squinting through the dust. The horses stamped and tossed their rough manes. Tonio could hear the jingling of metal and the creak of leather.

The leader trotted up to where Messer Nicolo was standing, and began to speak in his rough, jerking way. Tonio had learned some words of the Tartar speech. He understood the man when he waved his thick fist towards the moving domes.

'Bring the horse, Tonio,' said Messer Nicolo. He spoke as calmly as if he were asking Tonio to bring the green gondola to the steps of the Ca' Polo. 'And the gray mare with the packs. Leave your bow, Mar Sarghis. And leave yours, too, Marco.'

Messer Maffeo and Hans had already put down their bows. Tonio helped the round little German to mount. His horse was a tall one. One of the red boots waved unsteadily in the air before he got it across the horse's back.

Tonio on his chunky pony trotted along after the three Polos. Hans led the gray mare. The Tartar horsemen were all around them, pressing close to them, fingering their Venetian cloaks, poking at their saddle bags, grinning with their wide mouths. They held out their hard, dirty hands and asked for presents, chattering like a lot of inquisitive crows.

'Give us sharp knives, knives,' they kept saying. 'Bread, fine bread. Give us bread and cakes for our children.'

'When they're not stealing, they're begging,' muttered Mar Sarghis, scowling.

Messer Nicolo and Messer Maffeo seemed to know how to treat the Tartars. They spoke to them courteously without showing any signs of dislike or fear.

'Our gifts are for your lord, Barka Khan,' said Messer Nicolo quietly.

Tonio recognized the Khan's name. He knew that Messer Maffeo and Messer Nicolo had traded with that Tartar lord on their other journey.

Most of the white domes had stopped moving now. The Polos and the horsemen had almost reached the river. Tonio could see the trampled mud at the ford. Across it horses were drinking. Beyond them were oxen and goats and sheep, so many that Tonio could hardly see where the herds stopped.

The things that looked now more like great white beehives than like domes were really, Tonio saw, big tents of white felt. They were mounted on carts, carts as wide as the great banquet hall at the Ca' Polo. Men were unharnessing the oxen from the carts. Others were lifting off the tents.

Tonio caught sight of the wicker framework under the felt and of pictures of birds and beasts painted on the white doors.

At the top of each tent stuck up a round white chimney like a high collar. These felt chimneys were painted, too, with bright splashes of color. All around the great carts with the tents on them were smaller carts carrying chests covered with black felt. Women were pulling rugs, furs, and cooking things out of these chests. The women had queer high hats on their heads with feathers sticking out of them.

'The ladies look as big as their houses,' said Marco to Tonio. 'I can hardly tell one from the other!'

'Tartars like fat wives,' said Mar Sarghis, 'and the flatter their noses are, the better.'

'Then these must be very beautiful!' said Marco.

They were riding along now beside the city of tents. In the

middle of the south side of the felt and wicker city was a large empty space.

Messer Nicolo said over his shoulder to the boys: 'Watch now if you want to see a sight.'

Out of a fold in the rolling plain came a wagon bigger than any Tonio had seen. There were white oxen pulling it—two long rows of them—and a fat woman standing in the door of the house. She was shouting at the oxen and slashing a long whip above their backs.

Tonio began to count the oxen—'Eighteen, nineteen, twenty,' he said, counting with his fingers against his pony's hot neck. 'Two rows of ten across the front.'

'Twenty-two,' said Marco. 'Rows of eleven.'

'Twenty,' insisted Tonio.

'Well, anyway,' said Marco, 'it would fill up the whole Canal of San Giovanni Grisostomo, wouldn't it?'

'It would fill the Piazzetta!' said Tonio.

'Travellers' tales!' chuckled Messer Maffeo, turning his jolly red face towards the boys. 'It's the Khan's house,' he added. 'We must wait while they set it up, but it won't take long.'

The white oxen stamped along the dry ground, the huge wagon jolting behind them. Men walked along beside them shouting at them. The woman in the door shouted louder than ever. The oxen turned and backed the cart into the place of honor, the centre of the south side of the camp. Other men rushed forward and set the tent in its place. There was a great deal of shouting, of rushing about with bundles of rugs and shawls, while the Polos waited surrounded by a part of the Tartar horsemen.

When the Khan's tent was ready, one of the horsemen rode off among the grassy hills. In a few moments a party came out of the valley. The sun had set and in the dim light Tonio thought he saw soldiers with helmets and lances above them with fluttering scraps of color at their tips. A man on a white horse galloped ahead, threw himself off his horse, and walked stiffly towards the Khan's tent on short, bowed legs.

'Barka Khan himself,' said Messer Nicolo.

'And all his wives,' chuckled Messer Maffeo.

Then Tonio saw that what he had thought were soldiers with lances were really only more fat ladies with high feathered hats. They had bright blue scarfs covering the lower part of their faces, but above them Tonio could see that their noses were the flattest he had seen yet.

There was a cold, raw wind blowing across the camp. The Polos' party sat shivering in it watching men in greasy sheep-skin jackets lighting fires. Smoke began to blow into Tonio's eyes. He sat coughing, trying to fan the stinging smoke away. Tears kept rolling down his cheeks. It was getting dark now. The figures of the Tartars were black around the blazing fires. Horses neighed and whickered, cattle bellowed, sheep and goats seemed to be trying to find out which could make the most noise. There began to be smells of cooking meat, and shouts of singing and bursts of music from the tents. In front of Barka Khan's tent there were two fires burning brightly. A man stuck two spears beside them and tied a cord from one to the other.

'We shan't have to wait long now,' said Messer Nicolo. 'Do just what I do and be sure to hold your heads up and look cheerful whatever happens. They think looking sad or gloomy is bad luck. You know that, Mar Sarghis. Remember it. Take the packs off the mare and carry them. Hans, stay with the horses. Mar Sarghis, take the saddle bags.'

Messer Nicolo jumped off his horse and slung his crimson leather saddle bags to the big Tyrian. Mar Sarghis took them and, looking far from cheerful, stood beside his own horse.

'You'll have to do better than that,' said Messer Maffeo, thumping Mar Sarghis on the shoulder.

'I'll grin like a frog when the time comes,' promised the Tyrian.

'What are the fires for?' asked Marco.

'We walk between them so that we can be clean enough to go into the Khan's presence, though we're cleaner now than these brutes would be if they had their skins burnt off them!' growled Mar Sarghis. 'Don't put your sword anywhere near the flames. They say it's bad luck. And if you do anything unlucky, you'll never see Venice again. Step clear of the threshold of the tent too...'

'Quiet! Here they come!' said Messer Nicolo.

Mar Sarghis raised his black head in its black fur cap and fixed his wide mouth in something that Tonio hoped the Tartars would know was a smile. The little party followed two Tartars between the two fires. They were so close together that Tonio felt as if his legs were going to be scorched.

At the door of the tent were two more Tartars in loose red robes. Messer Nicolo handed them his sword. The others did the same. The guards felt under the arms of the Venetians to be sure they had no weapons concealed.

'The threshold! Don't touch the threshold,' they kept saying, holding back the painted felt door so that the visitors could step in.

Inside the tent it was hot and smoky. A fire burned in the middle of an open space. Some of the smoke was going out the hole in the roof, but most of it hung about inside and made Tonio's eyes keep watering.

Near the door he saw a bench set with silver and gold cups and jugs. At the back of the tent was a sort of bed with three steps leading up to it. On the bed, surrounded by bright-colored cushions, sat the Khan.

No one spoke. The Khan in his satins and soft furs looked out of his bright little eyes through the smoke at the Polos. He seemed to have neither eyelids nor lashes, only the darting black eyes in the broad coppery face with its flat nose and wide mouth.

'Come forward,' he said at last.

Messer Nicolo moved a few paces towards the Khan, knelt down, bowed his head, got up again. The others followed him, Messer Maffeo with a good deal of difficulty, Mar Sarghis still with his fixed smile. After a great deal of kneeling and bowing, the little party stood in front of the Khan's seat.

There was a good deal of gold about it, and there were beautiful embroideries hanging behind the Khan. His bows and quivers hung at his right hand. Near them was a hideous little image of felt and feathers with a face as flat and blank as any Tartar's. The fattest of his wives sat at his left hand and stared at the Polos above her blue scarf. Her nose looked as if it had been pared off with a knife.

When Messer Nicolo and Messer Maffeo finally stood before the Khan, he stopped his cold staring and began to smile and talk so fast in the Tartar language that Tonio could not understand him. He saw, though, that Barka Khan remembered the Polo brothers and was glad to see them.

'Open the pack, Tonio. Give me the saddle bags, Mar Sarghis,' said Messer Nicolo.

He and Messer Maffeo spread out presents on the steps of the Khan's seat: a purple robe of Venetian velvet, a girdle of gold cords and scarlet silk, a helmet inlaid with patterns of gold. And from the crimson saddle bags Messer Nicolo pulled out little packets and began to pour at the Khan's feet the things that Tonio had seen in Messer Giacomo's shop.

The Khan bent forward over the bright necklaces and bracelets and rings. He was evidently pleased, for he gravely fitted a dozen rings onto his stubby fingers, and scooped up everything into a bright heap beside him. He threw his wife a string of Venetian beads. Her bright little eyes flashed with pleasure.

Barka Khan waved to the men near the bench. They began to fill the gold and silver cups. The musicians started to twang and bang on their instruments. The cupbearers came around with their full cups, held them out to the Venetians, and then, when the visitors were about to take them, drew the cups back. Messer Nicolo and Messer Maffeo laughed, tried again to take the cups. At last, after a great deal of offering and snatching back, and much yapping laughter from the Tartars, the visitors were allowed to drink. The stuff burned Tonio's mouth and made his head sing, but it left a pleasant taste in his mouth,

like that of almonds. He would have liked more, but no one offered him any. At last, after much noise, dancing, singing, and eating of half-cooked meat, the Polos were allowed to go back to the caravan.

'I think we have done a good day's business,' said Messer Nicolo as they rode along.

'It ought to be good,' grumbled Messer Maffeo. 'I have nearly broken my poor old back bowing to our friend. Did you hear my knees creak, Marco, when I went down the third time?'

'I heard them snap like bowstrings,' laughed Marco. 'But

why is this such good business, father? Surely you've given away most of your jewels and have got nothing in return.'

'As to that,' said Messer Nicolo, 'we'll see later.'

CHAPTER 9

PIETRO

THE CARAVAN went on the next day, but the Polos stayed at Barka Khan's camp for several weeks. Marco and Tonio got to know some of the Tartar boys about their own age. They went hunting with them and learned to play their games. The Tartars were wonderful shots with their bows. Marco and Tonio spent hours with them practising shooting. Tonio improved, but he never shot so well as even the poorest of the Tartar boys. Marco, however, became as good a shot as any but the very best of them.

Tonio said Marco was better than any Tartar, but Marco only laughed at him. 'Pietro shoots twice as well,' Marco said. Pietro—as Marco called him because his Tartar name sounded rather like that—was a tall, slender boy with strong, wiry arms. His face was wide and flat like those of the other Tartars, but his eyes had a gentle look and he had a pleasant way of smiling. He rode his horse so well that you could hardly tell which was horse and which was boy. He could shoot from the moving horse better than Tonio could from his feet. He could even turn in the saddle, shoot an arrow backwards, and hit a small mark.

Pietro had no father and mother—only an older brother who beat him a good deal. Pietro took the beatings as he did everything else—quite cheerfully. As long as he had his horse and plenty of arrows to shoot, he was perfectly happy.

One day when Marco and Tonio went to find Pietro, their friend had disappeared. He was nowhere near his brother's tent. The brother only grunted rudely at Marco when he asked where Pietro was. Marco and Tonio wandered about the camp looking for Pietro. It was in front of the Khan's own tent that they found him at last. He was kneeling down in the dirt with his clothes torn off his back. A big Tartar with a long-lashed whip was standing over the boy. Barka Khan was looking on out of the bright eyes that seemed to prop up their bare lids and smiling cruelly. Pietro did not look at his friends. His mouth was shut tight and his head was held up straight. He was looking across the plain where the sheep were eating.

The big Tartar made his whip whistle through the air and brought it down on Pietro's bare back, but the boy never moved. Marco ran forward to Barka Khan. The young Venetian was on friendly terms with the Tartar lord, partly on Messer Nicolo's account, partly because of Marco's own skill at sports.

'If you please, my Lord,' said Marco, kneeling down and looking up into Barka Khan's face with his shining gray eyes, 'this boy is my friend. Will you tell me why he is being lashed?'

'Your friend is a thief, Messer Marco,' said the Khan, with a short, yapping laugh. 'We don't allow thieves in our camp. He has stolen another boy's arrows. They were found among his things. A hundred lashes is the punishment.'

The lash descended on Pietro's back again, but the Tartar boy made no noise.

'My Lord,' said Marco hastily, 'I have heard that such offences can be paid for. Whatever Pietro has done, let me pay for it.'

The Khan waved his fat hand sharply towards the man with the whip.

'Let the boy get up,' he said, 'if Messer Marco will answer for him.'

The affair was finally settled by Marco's paying the owner of the arrows ten times their value. Pietro, who had never even moaned during the whipping, burst into tears when he saw the sulky-looking Tartar carrying off Marco's best knives, strings of Venetian beads, and scarlet cloth. Messer Nicolo had given both Marco and Tonio goods for trading with the Tartars. This was Marco's first bargain.

'I never stole the arrows, Messer Marco,' Pietro sobbed. 'I am not a thief. Oh, believe me, I wouldn't steal! They were put there by someone who hates me because I hit the target when he missed.'

'I believe you, Pietro,' said Marco. 'Let's not talk any more about it.'

After that Pietro was never far away from Marco. He brought Marco presents—skins of foxes he had killed, arrows that he had made, a pair of fine horsehide boots, a young falcon that he had trained. He taught Marco all his own tricks of shooting and riding, and seemed his happiest when Marco shot as well as he did.

Marco and Tonio could not spend all their time shooting. Messer Nicolo and Messer Maffeo were busy trading with the Tartars and the two boys had to keep account of the Venetian goods—the jewels, mosaics, and beads—and the things received in return for them. For a long time Barka Khan offered nothing in exchange for the jewels the Polos had brought him, but when the Venetians began to get ready to leave the camp, it was his turn to give presents.

The tent that he had given the visitors for their use was filled with pieces of silk, furs, bags of gold, and silver-mounted saddles and bridles. To each of the Polos he gave double robes with foxskins inside and out. To the rest of the party, he gave heavy leather breeches and jackets of sheepskin. Outside the tent were fresh horses for their journey and food for many days. There were skin bags of koumiss—that queer drink made of mare's milk that tasted like almonds. There was honey, dried meat, bags of garlic, and the salted tail of a fat sheep. Some of the Tartar sheep had tails so heavy that they had to be carried in little carts behind them. This one weighed twelve pounds, and was, Tonio thought, about the worst form of food he had tried yet. The Tartars, however, considered it a splendid present.

Barka Khan sent an escort of his best horsemen to help the Polos on their road. Everyone in the camp crowded around to say good-bye. Marco and Tonio rode among them giving some last presents—beads, sweetmeats, small knives. The flat faces

were all smiling now; all except one, that is. On the very edge of the crowd stood Pietro, looking sad and lonely.

Marco rode back to the Khan and made him a polite speech of thanks for the splendid coat of fur and the fine new saddle on which he was riding. Marco spoke the Tartar language well now. The Khan seemed pleased with his speech.

'Ask me for whatever you like,' he said. 'You shall have it.'

Marco hesitated a moment. Then he pointed his scarlet whip at the lonely figure of Pietro.

'Let me take my friend there with me, my Lord,' he said.

Barka Khan gave one of his sharp, yelping laughs.

'Oh, the thief!' he said. 'Take him by all means. We can do without him very well!' He shrugged his shoulders and said to Messer Nicolo: 'Your son will never make a merchant. I would have given him a robe of sable if he had asked.'

Messer Nicolo smiled.

'A friend by your side can keep you warmer than the richest furs, my Lord,' he said. 'Your friendship, as well as the fine robes you have given us, will help to warm us on our journey. I think my son has made a good bargain.'

Messer Nicolo was right. It was not long before Pietro proved to be the best gift that Barka Khan had made them.

The little party, seven of them now with Pietro, and the twenty horsemen of their escort, rode off eastward in the cold morning sunshine.

Pietro was fitted out like the other Tartars.

'I was all ready to go,' he told Tonio, a happy smile now on his broad face. 'I hoped he'd take me.'

He had two long bows and three quivers of arrows, an axe, a coil of rope, a crooked sword, a wicker shield covered with leather, and a leather bag of food. His shaggy horse had on a coat of leather, covered with small plates of polished steel. Pietro himself was dressed in a leather jacket lined with ram's wool, leather breeches, and high boots. He had an iron helmet on his head held by a band of leather under his chin. His jacket had a fur-lined hood that he could pull over the helmet. He smiled out from under the helmet at Tonio and Marco every time he looked at them. Now and then he climbed up on his horse's back and balanced on it as it pounded along. At other times he flung himself down off one side of his horse and squirmed up on the other without touching the ground, still smiling happily. The horse seemed to be quite used to these tricks and jogged along calmly whatever his master did.

The party travelled much faster than the caravan could go, but the days were short and the nights long. They slept under the stars, sometimes finding themselves covered with snow in the morning. Tonio grew fond of the Tartar guards. The men were always cheerful, no matter how hard they had ridden, how little they had eaten, or how cold and wet they were. All the Polos were sorry when they reached the mud-walled city of Tauris with the red mountain behind it and said good-bye to their guides.

'You have brought us so fast that we have caught the spring itself,' Marco said to the Tartar captain. 'I am sorry you have to ride north into the snow again.'

It was true that they had travelled south so quickly that

they had come to a warmer country where there was no snow. There was hot sand instead with red rocks sticking out of it.

The Tartar gave one of his short, yapping laughs.

'I'd rather ride with Barka Khan with my feet frozen and an empty food bag than sit on cushions all day in Abagu Khan's palace. Yes, even if they gave me two silver pitchers of koumiss to drink every day and a boy to pour it into a gold cup for me,' he said. 'Take care of yourself, Messer Marco. May your horse never stumble. May your arrow fly straight to the mark.'

He waved his hand to his men, and tightened his reins. The troop wheeled and rode off in a cloud of red dust.

CHAPTER 10

GOLDEN APPLES

SPRING HAD come to Tauris, and the sun shone hot on the red mountains and the mud walls of the city. Its ruler, Abagu Khan of Persia, was a Tartar, but he did not live in a tent. His palace in Tauris was in the middle of gardens where fruit trees were in blossom. He sat in a high, dimly lighted room with a ceiling of deep blue and with gold on the walls. He accepted the Polos' presents, but in a sulky way that made the whole party uneasy. Tonio, carrying the heavy pack, stumbled at the door and came within an inch of stepping on the threshold. The shouts of the guards and the scowl that the Khan turned on the boy made him shiver.

The room to which they were shown for the night was small and hot. Tonio slept badly. Once when he woke he found that Pietro was gone. Tonio was still awake when the Tartar came back. The rest of the party slept heavily.

'We must not stay here,' Pietro whispered. 'These Tartars

are getting ready for war. I have been to the camp and talked with the soldiers. They are all talking about it. Some say that Abagu Khan will fight against the Great Khan himself. If there is war no one will be afraid of the gold tablets. This is no place to trade. We must go tomorrow.'

In the morning Tonio told Messer Nicolo what Pietro had heard. Messer Nicolo listened to what both boys had to say, but he only shook his head.

'It would be foolishness to try to go alone,' he said. 'We must wait until they give us an escort.'

But no escort was given. Abagu Khan only looked sulkily at the golden tablets of Kublai Khan. The Polos would have to wait, he said. The party waited for many days while every day troops of horsemen left the city galloping eastward. Messer Nicolo was bold enough to ask to go with one of these troops, but the Khan still scowled and told them to wait.

Abagu Khan had a son, Prince Argon, a boy about as old as Marco. He was a handsome young prince, with stiff reddish hair, a cheerful red face, and round blue eyes. He was very different-looking from most of the Tartars except for his short thick nose and wide cheekbones. Prince Argon was as fond of shooting as any of the Tartars and very skilful with his bow. He used his left hand and was as swift and lively as a young fox. One day he invited Marco to a shooting match.

There were crowds of people around the flat piece of ground near the camp where the match took place. At one end of the field were set up two tall posts with a thin bar resting on their tops. To this bar were tied ten cords. At the end of each cord was an apple—five silver apples and five gold ones.

Marco had brought Tonio and Pietro with him. They looked on while the young princes, Argon's brothers and cousins, rode through the posts under the dangling apples, turned in their saddles, and, shooting back from their moving horses, tried to hit the cords with their arrows. Prince Argon shot far better than anyone else. He shot down five apples—three gold and two silver. One of his cousins, Baron Coja, a jolly thin young man, hit two. No one else had more than one.

There were two boys standing near Prince Argon's seat, one with a dish of sugared fruits and cakes, another with a jug of koumiss. The Prince kept eating and drinking after each shot. After he had eaten most of the cakes, he remembered his visitor. The boy brought the plate over to Marco. There were a few broken cakes and some raisins on it. Marco took a few raisins, but he refused the cup of koumiss that the other boy offered him.

'Prince Argon,' said the boy, 'asks you to speak to him.'

Marco got up and, followed by Pietro and Tonio, walked over to the place where Prince Argon was. The Prince looked very hot and red. He was half-lying on a broad marble bench with a piece of cloth of gold wrinkled up under him. He was teasing a fluffy black cat with one of his golden apples, pulling it along the ground just in front of the cat's darting topaz eyes and jerking it away from the black velvet paws. His handsome face had a cruel look on it.

At first he paid no attention to Marco, but went on playing with his golden apples, and drinking out of his jewelled cup whenever it was held out to him.

Marco knelt down before the Prince. Tonio and Pietro knelt a little behind him. All three were wearing Venetian clothes. Tonio had given one of his suits to Pietro, so that they were both in red tunics with the Polo coat of arms embroidered on them. There were small pebbles where they were kneeling.

They could all feel them grinding through their thin Venetian hose and bruising their knees. Tonio almost groaned. If there were holes in the stockings, he would have to mend them. Aunt Bella had taught him how and rapped his fingers when they were clumsy. They had been rapped pretty often!

Pietro looked very odd in his Venetian cap, with his black hair braided and looped around his ears in the Tartar fashion.

At last Prince Argon rolled over on the bench and sat up. He kicked the cat away and yawned.

'Did you ever see such shooting as mine?' he asked sharply, stretching his strong arms.

'It was splendid shooting, Prince,' Marco said politely. 'I thank you for inviting me to see it.'

'The best shooting you've ever seen?' insisted the Prince, his face turning even redder than before.

'Why,' said Marco, still speaking politely, 'I have seen so many wonderful tricks with arrows since I have met your people that it is hard to say that one is better than another, but certainly what I have seen today is among the best. It must be very hard to hit those cords. Some day I must try it.'

Tonio heard Pietro give a gasp. Pietro knew that Prince Argon would not like Marco's honest way of speaking. Tonio thought for a moment that Prince Argon was going to swing his golden apple at Marco's head.

'You try it!' The Prince gave a short, rude laugh, and snapped the strong fingers of his left hand. 'If the three of you together can bring down half as many apples as I can, I'll give you—Why, what shall I give you? Diamonds? Rubies? Gold? Say what, Venetian.'

'Twenty of your soldiers, my Lord, to help us on our journey,' said Marco.

The Prince laughed again—a laugh like a fox's bark.

'That is easily given,' he said, 'even if you earn them. If you do not, you must stay and entertain me. A nice long visit.'

Tonio did not like the look with which Prince Argon spoke of that long visit. He was afraid it would be spent behind the mud walls of the prison near the Khan's palace—as dirty and gloomy-looking a building as he had ever seen.

The Prince drank again from his jewelled cup.

'My horse,' he said, snatching up his bow and clicking his long thumb nail against the taut string.

The grooms brought up a black horse that kicked at them and reared.

More apples were hung up. All gold ones this time.

Prince Argon flung himself on the black horse. He had on thin white clothes and on his red hair a cap with an emerald in it. His eyes looked very blue and keen in his red face. The horse pranced and wheeled about, but calmed down at Argon's voice and the touch of his hand on the reins. In a moment the Prince let them fall on the horse's neck, and made him move fast or slow, turn and wheel, just with the pressure of his knees against the scarlet-and-gold saddle. But this time the Prince did not shoot so well as he had before. When he had dashed between the posts ten times, there were still six apples gleaming in the spring sunshine.

The Prince made Tonio go next—snapped his fingers at him and laughed his fox's bark again. Tonio rode back and forth on his hot, shaggy pony, but none of his arrows brought down an apple. One arrow almost grazed one of the apples, but that was the nearest he came. It was hard to go back to his place with the Tartars laughing at him.

'His head is the only apple of gold *he'll* ever have,' he heard one of the young princes say to Baron Coja.

The Baron came up to Tonio and spoke kindly to him. 'You would soon learn the trick,' he said. 'It is hard to learn in a strange place.'

'I'm afraid I should never learn anywhere,' said Tonio.

Marco came next. He missed his first two shots, but the arrow flew close to the cord.

'Surely he'll hit it next time,' thought Tonio, but the next shot went even wider. In all his ten shots Marco brought down only one apple.

'Two's half of four, Pietro,' Marco said, smiling at the young Tartar. 'You can do it for us. Steady now.'

Pietro did not smile back. Tonio saw that the young Tartar's hand was shaking. He missed his first three shots while the crowd laughed at him.

Pietro stopped beside Marco. His horse was panting and so was he.

'If I do not hit it,' he muttered, 'ride off quickly before they take you prisoner. If they take me, no matter. Go to your father. He has the tablets of Kublai Khan. They will obey him—for a while.'

Marco only smiled at him.

'Never mind about that, Pietro,' he said cheerfully. 'You'll hit it. You're better than any of them.'

Pietro dropped his rein on his fat little horse's ragged mane.

'Fly straight now, old fellow,' he whispered, patting the horse on the neck.

The chunky brown horse thudded off down the dusty field, and under the shining apples. Pietro swung in the saddle. An arrow whizzed out of the dust cloud. There was a moving flash of gold as an apple fell with its cord neatly cut.

Marco ran over to him.

'We've won, Pietro! You did it! Splendid!' Pietro grunted.

'I don't call that winning,' he said.

'Why, yes, it is. He said we couldn't knock down half as many apples as he could. Two's half of four, Pietro, so we've done it.'

Pietro only grunted again.

'I haven't finished,' he said, and whirled his horse around. There had not been much applause when Pietro's apple fell. Prince Argon was angry at losing his bet. He had only looked sulkily at the fallen apple and the rest of his party had copied him. And when the second apple fell, the crowd was still silent, except for the young Baron Coja who gave a friendly shout of 'Well shot, boy! Well shot!'

But when the third arrow cut the cord there was a murmur of praise from all the princes. When the fourth apple flashed and fell there was clapping of hands and stamping of feet.

Then there was silence, a silence in which the beating of the horse's feet was like thumping on a great drum. Tonio saw Pietro's crimson figure swing in the saddle. He heard the snap of the string and the singing of the arrow. The apple fell with a little thud and the whole crowd around the big field roared and stamped and clapped. Pietro had shot as well as the Prince himself had ever done.

'Five apples in a row! That's shooting for you!' yelled one of the young princes. Baron Coja jumped in the air, waving his cap.

Prince Argon came forward. He did not like losing, but he was good sport enough to admire fine shooting when he saw it.

'Take the apples,' he said, swinging them by their cords into Pietro's arms. 'You shall have your soldiers, Messer Marco. But let me ask you a favor in return. Leave me this fine bowman here, who shoots better than I do.'

'He is free to stay if he likes,' said Marco, 'but I have promised to take him to the Great Khan. I must keep my promise to him if he chooses to go.'

Prince Argon frowned and shrugged his broad shoulders, but Kublai Khan's name was still powerful enough so that he did not insist on Pietro's staying in Tauris.

To stay there was the last thing Pietro wanted. He thanked the Prince for his kindness, but rode off after Marco with the golden apples swinging from his saddle bow.

'What a fine trade I made with Barka Khan!' said Marco, patting Pietro's hot shoulder.

CHAPTER 11

FOG IN THE DESERT

'WE MUST go south to Hormuz,' said Messer Nicolo. 'If what Pietro says about a great Tartar war beginning is true—and everything I see makes me think he's right—we shall be safer to go by sea.'

Everyone was glad to think of travelling by water again. Tonio had seen all he wanted to see of horses and camels for a while. He was tired of jolting over the sandy deserts of Persia. He was homesick for the cool ripple of the tide at night and the swift skimming of his gondola by day.

The days grew hotter and hotter as they got nearer to Hormuz. Messer Maffeo grumbled about the heat and told them about a whole army that was burned to death by a hot wind when it was coming to attack Hormuz.

'Right across the desert they came,' he said. 'The people in the city waited for them with their swords and bows ready. After a while they got tired of waiting and went out to look for the enemy. They were in rows. All baked like loaves in an oven. If I have to ride much longer in this sun, I'll be baked too.'

Messer Maffeo groaned loudly, but looked more cheerful than anyone else.

'Wait till I get to the city,' he said. 'I'll get into a jar of water up to my neck and sit there all day. If there's a jar big enough!'

Marco laughed at the idea of his uncle's sitting in a jar of water with his black curly beard and jolly red face sticking out of it, but Messer Maffeo said that people in Hormuz really did get into water in hot weather, when the wind blew across the desert, and they would stay there till it stopped even if it blew all day.

Rich men had pools and tanks in their gardens outside the city. Poorer ones really used the big oil jars.

'The kind, you know, Tonio,' said Messer Maffeo, 'that the forty thieves once hid in. Only I never believed that story till I saw these jars.'

The really poor people ducked into the river or the harbor when the dust storms came.

They rode on towards the city. There was a haze of heat and dust quivering over it. The walls and the domes and the towers were only shadows in the dusty air. Tonio could hardly tell which were the domes and which were the dark clouds piled up behind them. The heat and bad smells of the city seemed to be steaming out of it. There was a river, but it was so dry that there was only a trickle of water in the shadow of the date palms along the banks. Wherever the palm trees made a little shade, the water was dark with black heads and splashing brown arms. These people lived in huts made of dried palm leaves.

Inside the city the narrow streets were empty. Baking heat from brick and plaster walls filled the dark alleys. Here and there a ragged beggar slept in the shadow of a doorway.

'Where are all the people?' asked Tonio.

'Where I told you,' said Messer Maffeo. 'In the water.'

The house where the Polos stopped was built of bricks with yellow plaster over them. The walls felt like the walls of an oven. The windows were narrow slits that let in the smallest possible amount of light. It was cooler inside, but stuffy and smelling of garlic and salt fish.

The rooms were small. 'Like cells in the Doge's prison,' Messer Maffeo grumbled.

There were strange animals painted on the walls. It was so dark that Tonio could not see whether they were lions, or birds, or both.

The master of the house—he was a merchant whom Messer Nicolo and Messer Maffeo had visited in Hormuz before—was in the garden. The servant took them there. They found him in the pool with his head sticking out of the water, just as Messer Maffeo had said. He was a Venetian who had lived in Persia so long that he had almost forgotten how to speak his native tongue. He remembered enough of it, however, to invite the travellers to share his pool. Marco and Tonio were soon splashing and ducking each other as happily as if they had been on the beach of the Lido.

The merchant told them that it wasn't a very hot day.

'Just fine summer weather,' he said with a smile.

When he came out of the water he put on a red Persian robe.

'As if it weren't hot enough already!' Marco said.

Towards evening it grew a little cooler. The Polos walked through the stifling streets to the market place. There were all sorts of people there: flat-faced Tartars, Jews with long beards, dark-skinned horse dealers from southern India talking with tall, pale-faced ones from Persia. Once Tonio saw a short little man with slanting eyes in a yellow face smiling politely up at a tall Arab. The Arab in his flowing white robe looked about twice as tall as the plump little man in the silk coat. After a good deal of scowling and growling from the Arab, during which the yellow man smiled and bowed as if he could not stop, the big man dropped some gold pieces into the fat yellow hand and pushed off through the crowd.

"'Civil words pay all they cost,'" quoted Marco from the Merchant's Rhyme. 'Now, where does that funny little man belong, Uncle Maffeo?'

'In Cathay,' Messer Maffeo answered.

Marco and Tonio both gazed after the little man in the plum-colored silk.

Cathay! That smiling face might have looked at Kublai Khan!

They slept on the housetop that night with their faces turned towards the east. When the sun came up in the morning, it seemed to shoot up right out of Cathay.

One day their merchant friend came into his garden with his hands behind him.

'I have here,' he said, smiling, 'the thing you will say is the best in all Hormuz. So what is it, you clever fellows?'

'Pearls,' said Tonio.

'Salt fish,' laughed Marco.

The merchant shook his head.

'Only paper,' he smiled. 'Just a dirty old bag of paper. But I think a piece of it has your name on it, Messer Marco.'

'Letters!' said Marco. 'Letters from Venice! I'm right! I know I am!'

So he was. Among the many business papers for his uncle and father there was a thick roll of parchment with Messer Marco Polo on it in fine black letters. It was from Aunt Bella.

'My dear nephew Marco,' the letter said. 'Sometimes I wish women could learn to write, but as your Uncle Maffeo so kindly says, "Women and monkeys can learn tricks, but although a monkey dresses in silk it is still a monkey"; so, though I cannot write to you with my own hand, I can still use my tongue and our good priest Pietro Pagano of San Felice holds the pen and does his best to keep up with me. We heard of Venetians going to Hormuz and we send our letters in case you are still there. I hope that you are all well and that you are careful not to stay out in the evening mists which have bad poisonous fevers in them. Do not eat too many sweets and be sure never to sit down in wet clothes.

'I suppose Tonio Tumba has spoiled his new suit long before now. Tell him that we have a new gondolier. The one who took Tonio's place first was lazy and stole ginger from my private cupboard. The present one is a most worthy man. He did me a great favor by returning the green gondola that Tonio left so carelessly at the Lido the day the fleet sailed. Rosa, who has not improved at all in her manners, told me to tell Tonio that the new gondolier was too fat to run. This is, of course, foolishness, as a gondolier's place is in his gondola—not chasing people with eels.'

'So she found that out, did she!' said Marco, laughing.

'However,' the letter went on, 'boys would be boys, and when Tonio comes home I will try to find a place for him. Helping the cook, perhaps—or with the fishmonger. The house has certainly never seemed so peaceful, Marco, as it does now since you two boys went away. It is a great thing to have a trustworthy gondolier.

'The Loredanos have built a new courtyard and new rooms around it. They have a new gondola too. Such airs as they put on. I suppose Messer Loredano will set up to be the Doge before we know it. Donata is always in mischief. Her mother goes out to too many balls and that nurse lets her run wild.'

There were many more pages of the letter, full of news about the family and neighbors.

'Be a good boy, Marco,' it ended. 'Don't forget that onions are good for colds. Don't bring home any Tartar wives. There are plenty of nice girls in Venice. I shall be looking out for one who is a good cook and obedient. Don't stay away too long, because, while it is pleasant to have a quiet house, it is dull at times.'

The letter ended with messages to Messer Maffeo and Messer Nicolo and a whole shower of blessings from every saint that either of the boys had ever heard of.

'It makes Venice seem farther away, somehow,' said Tonio. 'And I don't like the sound of that trustworthy fat gondolier who brought my gondola home. He sounds too much like one I've heard of before.'

'Well, we can't do anything about it from here,' Marco said. 'Plenty of time to attend to him when we get back from Cathay. If we ever get there.'

The next morning Marco and Tonio went with Messer Maffeo to the docks to find a ship that would take them to Cathay.

'This is the finest harbor in the world,' said Marco, 'but do they call these things ships?'

'They must have some better ones than these,' said his uncle. 'Why, I'd as soon start in a walnut shell as in one of those.'

But the Persians had no fine galleys such as the Venetian ones. No one would agree to take the Polos to Cathay. They could start from Hormuz, the sailors said, in a boat carrying horses to India and perhaps they would find a better ship there. Only they would have to wait several months in India because the wind would be wrong. The wind blew from the southwest for months. The Polos could not sail down along India with the wind blowing from the south all the time and just enough from the west to drive their boats ashore.

Messer Maffeo went back to his brother, much disgusted with the ships. So was Marco.

'They're the worst things you ever saw,' he said. 'No nails, father, except a few wooden ones. The planks are stitched together with twine they make out of the husks of nuts. Not a smear of pitch on them, but just some bad-smelling fish oil. No decks. Only one sail. They put the cargo in, cover it with horsehides, and put the horses they sell in India on top of the hides. That's a great way to travel!'

'I'd sooner go in Tonio's gondola,' roared Uncle Maffeo. 'And as for these sailors who can't sail unless the wind blows just right and are too lazy to row, why, one Venetian is worth thirty of them.'

'Still I think we had better wait here for a while,' said Messer Nicolo. 'This wind may bring in one of Kublai Khan's great ships from Cathay. We know that they sometimes come to this port. We have seen at least one of his subjects.'

The Polos waited while the days grew hotter and hotter, but no ship came from Cathay. They did not see the yellow-faced man again. They all grew very tired of waiting, tired of the heat and bad smells, sick of the salt fish and dates that seemed to be all that people ate. The water of the Persian Gulf was not like that of the sparkling Adriatic.

'It isn't water at all,' said Marco to Tonio one hot day. 'It's only a bowl of steaming soup. And the sun hurts my eyes. It's like brass on the water. And on the sand—I don't know what it's like on the sand. My head—'

He dropped down on a bench in the dark, hot room of their mud-walled house and put his head in his hands.

Tonio was frightened. This was not like Marco. Marco never complained about anything. He was as cheerful as his uncle, and, like his father, took whatever came calmly and quietly. When Marco looked up, Tonio saw that his friend's face was hot and red. Marco lay down on the bench breathing as if he had been running.

Tonio ran into the garden and found Messer Nicolo.

'There's something the matter with Marco,' he said. 'I think he has a fever.'

Marco had a very bad fever, indeed. For days they were afraid he would never get well. The Persian doctor came and looked at him. He wrote magic prayers on pieces of paper and told Messer Nicolo to soak the paper in water and then give Marco the water to drink. Messer Nicolo gave the water to Marco, but it did not seem to do him any good. He could not eat the food they brought him. Much of the time he did not know where he was. Tonio stayed with him at night, fanning him, bathing him, giving him water to drink, and listening to Marco's voice.

Sometimes the sick boy spoke in whispers so low that Tonio could not hear what he said. Sometimes he shouted and laughed like Uncle Maffeo. But mostly he talked in his own voice, only speaking rather fast. Over and over again Tonio heard him say the Merchant's Rhyme, beginning, 'Honesty is always best,'

only he would mix the lines up and go back over it again and again. Marco had been trading all along the road. He seemed to remember just what he had paid for every piece of silk, but the sum never seemed to come out right. Sometimes he would be figuring the cost of carrying goods and Tonio would hear him mutter: 'Tauris—five aspers at the gate. Three to the watchman. Half an asper on the bridge. That makes—I forget.' Then he would go over it again, and go on, 'A present to the Khan's porter—two aspers... three aspers at the caravanserai... The sum never seemed to end. Tonio's own head would grow dizzy over it. It was better when Marco thought he was shooting and playing games in Barka Khan's camp, or on the galley sailing to Acre.

Tonio carried Marco up on the roof at night where it was cool, and back into a dark room by day. Marco did not seem to know where he was. He talked to himself, not to Tonio. One night Marco seemed to know Tonio. He looked straight at him with eyes that looked very large in his thin face. Marco whispered something, and then said quite loud: 'Get the gondola, Tonio. Oh, it's pleasant today in Venice, isn't it? How cool the water sounds! It rings on the marble... No, Donata, you mustn't go fishing. I'll catch your fish for you. See, your fine dress is all spoiled. Yes, my Lord, I come from Venice. You have a fine port here—the finest in the world. Except one. If the world were a ring Hormuz would be the pearl in it, but... Well, I'll tell you what it's like—our city. The sea's the street there. All green and cool. The houses dance in it. And the pigeons. They make a cool wind with their wings.'

He went on in whispers for a minute, so low that Tonio could not hear.

'Prince Argon had gold apples and hair like red-gold,' he

said, louder, 'but it's not so bright as a little girl's hair in Venice. A funny little girl. Playing in the sand. You see, the road to Cathay is very long. And it's all through sand—hot sand.'

The doctor and Messer Nicolo came in and stood looking down at Marco's thin face and arms.

'He cannot live in this heat,' the doctor said, in a low tone to Messer Nicolo. 'Your only hope is to get him up into the hills where it is cooler.'

'Can he stand the journey?' asked Messer Nicolo anxiously.

'As well as he can to lie here. Besides, you have been generous to me, sir, so I must tell you something else. If he should die in this city, the Governor will seize all his goods. It is the custom, and I can promise you that the Governor will think all your goods belong to your son. If you can prove they are yours, all right. But they'll take them first. If you get them back, you'll be surprised how few they were! Start tomorrow evening. There is a caravan going north. Get him to the hills.'

The journey to the hills saved Marco's life, but it was a long time before he was well again. His bed was put onto an oxcart covered with heavy silk curtains to keep off the sun. He seemed better almost as soon as they began to travel. He would ask Tonio questions about the places through which they passed.

'What is the name of this place, Tonio? What do they make here? What do they eat? What kind of money do they use? Is that the church? Oh, Tonio, is that a melon? Get me one, will you? I think I could eat a melon, and one of those peaches. Why, it tastes like a peach in Venice! Have one, Tonio. They're splendid peaches.'

Sometimes Tonio and Pietro rode beside the oxcart. Sometimes they walked, for they travelled very slowly now. Sometimes the Polos could hardly keep up with the slow-moving caravan. Marco could not go far in a day. He still had fever. It came on in the late afternoons. He would be burning with it one minute and shivering the next.

They had travelled sixty miles when they came to a hot, sandy desert. Mar Sarghis did not want to cross it.

'It would be better to leave the caravan and go around it,' he said to Messer Nicolo.

'Why do you say that, Mar Sarghis?' asked Messer Nicolo.

'Because of the Karuanas,' said the guide.

Marco heard the new word. He pushed aside the curtains and shoved his hollow-cheeked white face between them.

'Now, what are Karuanas, Mar Sarghis?' he asked excitedly.

'Enchanters, Messer Marco, who live in this desert. The other guides all say that they can make darkness come on in the daylight and that in the darkness they will ride in and seize us, take our goods, and sell us for slaves. I've been sold as a slave once too often,' said the Tyrian.

Marco laughed. 'You know you don't really believe that goblin tale, Mar Sarghis!' he said cheerfully. 'Let's cross the desert. I should like to see a Karuana. And it's the shortest way, isn't it, to the hills?'

It was the shortest way, and they took it, but everyone in the party, except Marco, felt uneasy. He did not see the places along the way where there were the bones of dead camels and horses—and of men. In one spot they found some bales of cloth torn open and thrown aside. Near a place where a fire had been made were the cooking pots and jars that had been left in the middle of a meal.

'People must have been in a hurry, to leave the good oil and grain behind them,' said Pietro to Tonio.

The word 'Karuanas' was often heard in the caravan. The

animals were urged on faster and faster. The camels and horses moved so quickly that the white humpbacked oxen that drew Marco's cart could not keep up with them. Hans, who was driving them, said that they could go no faster. The seven members of the Polos' party were left behind, the horses walking slowly along over the hot sand beside the silk-covered cart. The afternoon sun blazed down on their heads. Marco's fever came back. They could hear him talking to himself behind the curtains.

It was Pietro who said to Messer Nicolo: 'It's getting dark.' He spoke in a low, frightened tone.

Messer Nicolo looked up. There had been no clouds over the sun and there were no clouds in the sky now. The darkness seemed to be coming, not from the sky, but from the sand around them, like a dry fog. A few minutes before, the sun had been shining brightly on a sandy, rocky hill a little to the left of them. Now the hill had disappeared in the mist. So had the last of the caravan, though it was not far away.

Mar Sarghis turned a sort of greenish-yellow. He said to Messer Nicolo: 'We shall lose our way in the darkness.'

Even Messer Nicolo did not like the fog.

'We'll go to the hill we saw just now and wait there till it blows off. I hear a wind coming,' he said.

After some wandering about in the mist they found the hillside. There was a cave at the bottom of it enough for the oxcart. Mar Sarghis and Hans took shelter in it with the oxen, but Marco insisted on getting out. His teeth were chattering and his eyes were bright with fever. Tonio and Pietro wrapped him up and carried him to the top of the hill, stumbling over the rocks in the darkness. Marco was now very light. Tonio could have carried him alone on his back, he thought.

The mist was a little thinner on the hilltop.

'It will go soon,' Messer Nicolo said again. 'I hear the wind.'

'I don't feel it,' said Marco through chattering teeth.

No one else felt it either.

'It isn't wind,' said Pietro. 'It's horses' feet on the sand.'

They all knew that he was right. The sound of the hurrying hoofs grew louder and louder. It was below them now and they could see dim shapes through the mist, a whole wall of them, that flowed past the hill like a dark, thundering wave. It was gone in a moment and all they could see was the fog, but they could still hear the thudding rush of hoofbeats.

They all strained their ears. The drumming noise grew fainter. Then, just as it seemed about to fade away, there was more noise—a confused roar that they all knew was the sound of the helpless caravan being attacked in the darkness. The struggle lasted a long time. To the listeners on the hill it seemed like hours. Then it faded into the sound of hoofbeats again. They were not so swift this time, but there were more of them. The dark wave flowed past the hill again. It moved slowly with sobs and groans and harsh voices speaking the Tartar language. There was creaking of leather and jingling of metal.

When the mist burned off, there was no sign of either the Karuanas or their prisoners. The Polos hurried on towards a small village on the other side of the plain. Where the caravan had been, the sand was trampled with many hoof-marks. Someone had spilled a bag of cinnamon. It had been trodden on and its spicy smell hung over the place. Farther on they found a dead camel with a spear plunged into his side. No one had bothered to pick up his packs. Dates had tumbled out of them and were lying in the sand.

The caravan had vanished into the mist.

CHAPTER 12

HORNS IN THE SNOW

PIETRO AND Mar Sarghis argued about the Karuanas all through the pleasant valleys north of the desert. Mar Sarghis was surer than ever that the Karuanas were goblins who made the darkness. Pietro was just as sure that they were Tartars who made use of the dry fogs of that desert when they were lucky enough to find a fog and a caravan together. Tonio did not really care much about which was right. He was only glad to get away from that place, and to travel along eating pistachio nuts and walnuts, and buying fruit for Marco from the gardens along the way.

Marco ate pomegranates, oranges, grapes, and apricots as if he had never seen food before. By the time they came to Kerman, he felt strong enough to ride a horse again.

Kerman was a busy place on a dry plain with high hills around it. There were forts of sunbaked brick on the hills and brick-walled mosques whose domes made Tonio think of the domes of San Marco's Church in Venice. In the market place tall, fair-skinned Persians with spurs at their heels bought saddles and bridles trimmed with silver and blue turquoises. There were smoking forges around the town where smiths hammered fine steel into swords and shields.

In the houses the walls were covered with hangings, with birds and trees and flowers embroidered on them. Tonio slept with a silk cushion under his head and dreamed that he was chasing Rosa Polo down the Lido beach and throwing pink-and-blue pillows at her.

Marco and Tonio went into the market to help Messer Maffeo. He said, with his jolly laugh: 'I believe you get better bargains than I do, boys. You are getting to be real merchants. What do you think is the best thing in Kerman, Tonio?'

'Eels,' said Tonio, who was thinking of something else. 'No, I mean pink cushions.'

Marco laughed.

'Cushions stuffed with eels, I suppose you mean!' he said. 'Now those *would* be pleasant! What dreams you'd have!'

Tonio blushed. He wished he had not told Marco about that dream.

'I meant falcons,' he said. 'The red-breasted ones that fly so fast. See, the horsemen have them on their wrists.'

Marco looked at the Persian riders on their swift, long-tailed horses. The falcons had hoods of bright silk over their eyes. Around their legs were leather straps with bells on the ends. The bells made a silvery tinkling as the horses cantered through the dust. Tonio hoped Marco would think about the hunters instead of cushions full of eels. Tonio hated to be teased about being homesick.

However, Marco only said with a chuckle: 'Oh, you can chase things with falcons, too.'

Messer Maffeo did not make Tonio feel much better by grumbling: 'So you think it would be a good plan to take a few cages of these clawing, biting things, do you? You're not so clever as I thought, after all.'

In spite of Marco's teasing, however, and Messer Maffeo's good-natured scolding, Tonio was getting on in the world.

It took two camels now to carry Tonio's goods: four camels for Marco's. They joined another caravan—a bigger one with more guards.

The hills grew too steep for camels. They had to use asses. The Polos loaded the asses with wonderful embroideries. They traded some of their coral from Venice for turquoises as blue as the sky above the mountain passes. After they left Kerman, they were climbing all the time, higher and higher. The mountains all had snow on their tops. It was cold at night and they slept huddled close together. 'I'm glad I didn't throw away the fur coat Barka Khan gave me,' said Marco, shivering.

In a place called Balkh they camped in the ruins of a marble palace that Abagu Khan's soldiers had destroyed. Marco still had that fever that made him burn and freeze in the evenings. He had grown very tall, and he looked so thin that Tonio said he must be careful or someone would think he was a stick and break him up for firewood.

'A broomstick. And they'd break you with one hand,' agreed Uncle Maffeo in a cheerful roar.

They had built a fire in the hall of the old palace. The light of it turned broken marble columns pink. The smoke puffed out through a hole in the roof and covered a patch of night-blue sky and a few of the thousands of stars. One of the merchants of the caravan was standing beside the fire warming his cold hands. Marco kept shivering in spite of the warmth.

'You should take your nephew to Badakshan,' the merchant said to Messer Maffeo. 'I went there once with a fever I'd had a year and I lost it. This ruby I wear I got there, and I tell you since I've worn it I've never had a day's fever. The stone, you see, takes all the fever to itself.'

Marco looked into the deep red glow of the ruby.

'I should like to go to Badakshan,' he said, with his teeth chattering.

Whatever Marco wanted, his father and Uncle Maffeo wanted, too. No road was too rough or too narrow, no river too swift to cross, no mountain too steep to climb if it led to a place that might make Marco well. Sometimes it would take a whole day to get to the top of a mountain and almost as long to get to the bottom again. The horses here had no shoes on their feet. They scampered swiftly down hills—hills 'as steep as the sides of the bell tower in Venice,' Tonio said. The hills were full of flocks of wild sheep with twisted horns—horns

so big that people made bowls out of them.

At last they came to Badakshan. It was a beautiful plain with thick green grass on it and wonderful trees. Down the hills around it ran streams full of trout. The air was so clear that it took all the fever out of Marco's arms and legs, just as the merchant had said it would. Marco went fishing and hunting.

The men of Badakshan were fine archers, and he shot with them, but not for golden apples. He ran races with Tonio and Pietro. He ate enough for six boys. No one could mistake him for a broomstick now. His cheeks grew as red as his Uncle Maffeo's. When Marco glanced into the polished steel surface of his shield, he looked almost fat. He examined his face quite often in the mirror made by his shield because he hoped he would find that his beard had started to grow. He was often quite sure it had, but no one else seemed to notice it.

It was just before they left Badakshan that Marco found his rubies. Men dug them out of the mountains near-by, and there were plenty of them to be found, but none big enough and bright enough for Marco. He wanted three, he said: 'Good ones. I don't care anything about a quart of little ones.'

His father laughed at him.

'The Great Khan himself couldn't be more fussy about his rubies than my son here,' he said.

'What are you going to do with them, Marco? Wear two in

your ears and one in your nose?' bellowed Uncle Maffeo.

Marco shook his head. Tonio remembered the morning in the Church of San Marco. He thought he knew what Marco was going to do with them.

'Go to church and always spare
Him who sends thy gains a share,'
Tonio said in Marco's ear.

Marco smiled. He was sitting on a flat rock under a big walnut tree. Tonio and Pietro had unloaded one of the asses and spread out Marco's best pieces of silk and cotton cloth around him on the dry ground. The man who had dug the rubies laid a square of white silk on the rock. He kept putting small red stones on it. They were all too small. Marco kept shaking his curly brown head.

At last the merchant picked up a small packet. He swept the other rubies carelessly off the white silk and emptied the packet onto it. The sunshine that came through the walnut leaves blazed down on three great rubies. Tonio, standing behind Marco, gave a gasp. Marco pinched him hard in the calf of his leg. Tonio took the hint and was quiet.

'I sell them so cheap,' said the man, 'that it is like giving them away. I give you a present—' He named a price. Marco shrugged his shoulders.

'That present costs too much,' he said. 'It is not my father who is buying these. I am only just starting in business. Half what you ask is too much for me.'

'You want to rob me,' whined the man. 'My wife and children will starve.'

'That would be a pity,' said Marco, getting up and walking towards his horse. 'Well, I'll look somewhere else. I know that men find splendid rubies every day in these mountains. Pack up the goods, please, Tonio and Pietro.'

The man, tall, brown, with a leopard's skin over one shoulder, ran after Marco.

'Wait! I will ask my wife and see what she says.'

His wife was on the narrow mountain path beside a small donkey. She was padded out with yards and yards of cotton cloth to look as fat as possible. She almost filled the path and hid most of the donkey.

She nodded to her husband, and he came back smiling. The rubies were Marco's. He gave the merchant so many things that the little donkey could hardly stagger under his heavy load of coral and turquoises and cloth. His much-wadded mistress walked off happily with a bundle of embroidered quilts on her head. She looked strong enough to carry the donkey too. Tonio thought she would not starve right away!

Hans set the smallest ruby in a thin band of gold and fastened it to a gold chain. Marco wore it around his neck. The other two rubies no one saw after the day when they blazed in the sunshine under the walnut tree. Perhaps the red stone around his neck did not take Marco's fever away, but the merchant was right in saying that Marco would get well in Badakshan. Marco stopped burning and shivering after his visit to that pleasant place.

It did not seem as if there would still be higher mountains to climb, but there were, plenty of them. The nights grew longer and colder, but the travellers could go faster now that

Marco was well again. Before long they found themselves riding shaggy little horses on a plain covered with crusty snow between ranges of snowy mountains.

The older members of the party knew that dreary place well: 'The Plain of Pamir,' Mar Sarghis called it. The only track across it was marked by piles of the horns of wild sheep. Wolves had killed them. The curved points of the horns stuck through the snow. There were no birds, no trees—nothing but the wide sunny spaces of snow that dazzled their eyes and the dark mounds of horns that marked the trail. There was no noise but the sound of their own voices, the crunching of the horses' feet on the frozen snow, and the sudden howling of the icy wind.

It was Tonio's job to hollow out places in the snow at night for beds. Sometimes they found themselves with snow blankets over them in the mornings. Tonio was so cold one night that he could not sleep for a long time. The air was very crisp and still. The stars were as bright as the crystal of those goblets that were still being carried slowly towards Cathay for the Great Khan. Suddenly across that sky of deep blue, with its powder of silver stars, something seemed to rush. It was like the rush of the Karuanas through the fog.

'An army in the sky,' thought Tonio, 'with spears. There go the banners snapping in the wind; there go the horses galloping across the stars. Someone has a curved sword in his hand. He's waving it across the sky.'

Tonio spoke aloud without knowing it. Marco woke up, and the two boys watched the crackling waves of light dance above their heads.

'That,' whispered Marco, as the last snapping flags faded, 'is the finest thing I ever saw.'

Tonio chuckled and shut his eyes. The last thing Marco had seen was always the finest!

When they got up in the morning, they breakfasted on food that was only half-cooked. The water boiled, but seemed to have no heat in it.

Tonio saw Mar Sarghis rubbing the horses' gums with garlic.

'Why, it's true what you told Madonna Bella!' he exclaimed to Uncle Maffeo.

'Of course it's true!' roared Uncle Maffeo. 'But if I told in Venice half the things I know that are true, they'd chain me up for a crazy man.'

He tossed Tonio an onion.

'Eat that as you go along. It helps you to breathe this thin air.'

Tonio rode on, munching the raw onion. It seemed a long time since the day in the courtyard of the Polos' old house—'the gull's nest on the mud bank'—when he had heard Messer Maffeo telling his sister about Cathay and about rubbing garlic on horses' gums; the day that good San Nicolo had sent Hans to Tonio for a passenger; the day that Marco had given him his first gondolier's clothes.

Those clothes would not have covered half of Tonio now. He was as tall as Marco. His yellow hair was bleached straw-colored by sun and wind. There was a very faint yellow fuzz as soft as the down of the smallest chicken growing on his chin. Tonio felt very proud of it. He smoothed it with his fingers a good deal. Marco had noticed it, and was jealous. Marco had not yet found anything in his steel mirror that looked like a beard, and he was older than Tonio. And, of course, poor Pietro would never have a beard at all because he was a Tartar; at least, not a real beard—just a few wiry black hairs. All Pietro had so far were those skinny black braids of hair that he looped around his ears. Marco wanted to cut them off, but Pietro would not let him, although he would do anything else for Marco and followed him like a dog.

Far off across the snow Tonio heard a dog bark.

'I thought you said there were no animals on this plain in winter,' he said to Mar Sarghis. 'I heard a dog.'

The Tyrian scowled and listened.

'I wish it were,' he muttered.

Tonio heard that bark several times during the day. The horses were restless, but they moved slowly, panting hard in the thin, frosty air. Their breath was white in front of them and froze in tiny drops on their shaggy coats. Tonio's ears were cold in spite of the sheepskin hood over his head. The piles of horns of the dead sheep made a curved track. The travellers never seemed to get any closer to the snowy wall of mountains at the eastern end of the plain, no matter how many of these piles they passed.

It was colder than ever that night. Tonio scraped away snow so that the horses could eat the grass underneath. The party

huddled around a fire that flew about in the still air and gave almost no heat. They melted snow for water and drank it. The sun set in a clear sky, leaving the ring of snowy mountains pink around them. After the sun had been gone some time, one great peak turned a strange pale green like sea water in the moonlight. Then everything was dark, and in the stillness Tonio heard again that distant barking. The horses stamped nervously and stopped eating.

The men were talking around the fire. Only one of them heard what Tonio did. Pietro heard it, too. He beckoned to Tonio. They slipped away together into the silvery darkness outside the little circle of firelight.

'Your bow,' grunted Pietro. 'Get your bow.'

Tonio got it and his quiver and trotted after the Tartar's quickly moving figure. Pietro's bow and arrows were always close to his side. He carried a sharp spear in his left hand.

There was a big pile of the sheep horns not far from the camp; another pile, smaller, a little beyond it.

'We'll make a fort,' said Pietro, tugging one of the horns out of the snow.

Tonio helped him. They piled up the horns and heaped snow around them. The barking seemed nearer now. The moon came up over the eastern mountains. The barking changed to a howl that sent the boys to work faster than ever.

'Perhaps we ought to go back to the camp and tell them,' said Tonio, shivering a little.

'Too late,' said Pietro. 'Anyway, their ears will tell them pretty soon. Get down now behind the wall. Fix your arrow and don't shoot till I tell you to.'

He knelt behind the wall of horns and snow, fixed his arrow in the string, and stuck others into the snow in front of him.

Tonio did the same. Neither of them spoke, but Tonio thought his breathing must echo all over the Pamir Plain, it sounded so loud in his own ears.

'Coming,' said Pietro in the softest whisper.

The moonlight struck across the curved trail. There were dark figures moving down it—two, three—no, five. They were making no noise now, but padding silently along at a steady jog. They were coming straight down the track. Wolves!

'Take the one on the right!' Pietro said softly.

Tonio could see the wolves clearly now. The moonlight was shining on their frosty coats and cruel jaws. Their shadows were dark on the snow. The wind carried to the boys' ears the sound of soft feet crunching through the frozen crust.

'Now!' said Pietro.

The two bowstrings twanged together. The wolf on the right spun around growling and biting at Tonio's arrow. It had gone into his foot; Tonio had shot too low. Pietro's shot went true, and the black-and-gray figure in the middle went down with the arrow through his body.

The other wolves checked for a moment, barking furiously. Pietro shot again and another dropped on the body of the first. Tonio's fingers slipped on the string. His second arrow went wild just as the two untouched wolves bounded forward. They had seen the boys now and they came on snarling with dripping jaws. An arrow whizzed past Tonio's ear. One of the wolves bounded into the air with a terrible noise, half growl, half shriek, and fell backward against the other. The last wolf stopped for a moment, but that moment was enough. The boys shot again. Both arrows went true this time.

The air was full of howls from the dying wolves. Tonio heard quick footsteps and shouting behind them. The whole camp was coming: Messer Nicolo with a curved sword in his hand, Hans with an axe, Mar Sarghis with a club, Marco with a spear, Messer Maffeo puffing along in the rear with an iron spade—the only weapon he could lay hands on.

The wolf Tonio had wounded in the foot was limping off down the trail, travelling quickly in spite of the arrow broken off in the wound. It was Marco, running as swiftly as one of those soldiers he and Tonio had seen flickering across the sky, who killed the big brute with one clean thrust of his spear.

Messer Nicolo scolded the boys a little, but he smiled at the same time, so it did not seem much of a scolding.

'Next time you want to save our lives,' he said, 'just let us know your plans beforehand. We might,' he added, looking at his brother and chuckling, 'think it would be better to go after them with spades.'

Messer Maffeo laughed good-naturedly.

'With a spade,' he shouted, 'I'm a splendid archer!'

Pietro and Tonio, travelling across the roof of the world, had a wolfskin rug to sleep under on cold nights that winter.

CHAPTER 13

CATHAY AT LAST

'WE MUST be almost there,' said Tonio when they reached Khotan. There were fruit trees in bloom there. The people made wonderful carpets and fished lumps of jade out of the rivers. Tonio himself dived into the rushing waters and came out with a piece of white jade speckled with red—a piece fine enough for Kublai Khan himself, Hans said.

Tonio thought they must be near Cathay because now people spoke of it so often. From Khotan the Jade Caravan was starting for the Great Khan's court. The caravan went every three years and carried only the most beautiful jade—white, dark green, black, vermilion, green veined with gold. Kublai Khan was said to like the white-and-red kind best of all. Several merchants offered to buy Tonio's piece from him, but he kept it himself.

The Polos went with the merchants. Camels carried their packs now. The road the Jade Caravan took to Cathay was much longer than Tonio had thought. There were more mountains to climb, more rivers to ford, more snow, more floods, more mud holes, more heat—in fact, more of everything they had passed through already. There were more deserts—deserts as bad as the one near Hormuz. In the desert of Lop, Mar Sarghis said, there were talking spirits. It took a month to pass its hills and valleys of sand. The spirits tried to call people away from the caravan. They would make noises like the sound of a great army marching with drums and trumpets. Mar Sarghis warned them that people who tried to find that army would be lost in the sand hills.

Pietro as usual laughed at this talk of spirits, but Tonio noticed that he kept close to the rest of the party. The whole caravan moved slowly forward in a tightly packed mass. The animals all wore bells on their necks so that the caravan wound in and out among the hills of sand to tinkling music that shut out the queer noises. Messer Nicolo said that all the strange sounds were made by sand slipping and by the wind blowing in and out of the hot valleys. This seemed sensible to Tonio, but he wished that the bells on the camels' necks would keep ringing all night so that distant sounds of singing and wailing would not keep him awake. He was glad when a camel grunted and a bell tinkled in the darkness. Real sounds made the echoes of drums and teasing laughter keep still for a while.

Every night the leader of the caravan would put up a sign showing the direction of the next day's march. The trail was marked with the bones of men and of animals who had died along it. There was no water, no food. Only the miles of blazing sand that sometimes rose in clouds and cut their faces.

The desert ended at last. Nothing happened except that Messer Maffeo lost his spade.

'Just as I was getting to be such a good shot with it!' he said, with his jolly, roaring laugh. 'Oh, well, I'll get it on the way going home in a few years. I know just where I left it. Right behind sand hill number 999.'

After they left the desert, they began to travel through country where there were so many strange things that even Marco, who always noticed everything, could hardly remember them all. New things were always being added to the packs that the camels carried. There was the silky black-and-white hair of yaks—hair so long that Marco said no one in Venice would believe it if he didn't see it. Marco put a big roll of this hair into one of his bundles. Tonio took long feathers from the bright tails of pheasants. Messer Nicolo bought the finest cloth he had ever seen, woven from the hair of camels. Pietro shot a musk deer, and got the musk that the Venetians used in making perfumes. Pietro said he would take it to Venice and sell it on the Rialto, although he had no idea where the Rialto was. He asked Tonio and Marco all sorts of questions about their city.

Marco would always begin: 'Well, Pietro, it's the finest city in the world!'

'So I heard,' Pietro would say, with a wink at Tonio, and then all three boys would laugh, Marco as loudly as any of them.

At last they came to the country of Kublai Khan. Tonio was riding near Messer Maffeo when he heard a quick jingling of small bells somewhere ahead of them.

Messer Maffeo dug his heels into the fat sides of his horse.

'Listen, Tonio. We're in Cathay,' he said, and cantered forward.

Tonio followed him. The road curved sharply. Around the curve at a fork in the road was a building of stone with a queerly curved roof. Running towards it was a man with a leather girdle around his waist. Little bells, sewed to the girdle, jingled as he ran. As he came to the stone house, another man, with the same sort of girdle around his waist, snatched a roll of paper from the first runner's hand and started off along the other fork of the road.

'He runs as if a wolf were after him,' said Tonio.

'He's one of the Khan's messengers,' said Messer Maffeo. 'He will run three miles, as fast as he can go. Then another man will take the letter and run his three miles. A message

can reach the Khan in one day instead of ten. And here's one of the Khan's officers going to rob us.'

'Rob us?'

'Well, not exactly. He'll take all our gold and silver away from us and give us paper instead.'

'Everyone's money? *My* money?' asked Tonio. He had been carefully saving all the money that he had earned and sometimes getting some gold or silver in trade. He could not bear the idea of losing his coins and his wedges of gold and silver.

'Cheer up,' said Messer Maffeo. 'It's the same for everyone, and when we leave the Kingdom we'll leave the paper behind us.'

After a great deal of weighing and figuring, the Polos' party found themselves with their pouches full of those same yellow bank notes with the red seals that Hans had showed Tonio so long ago in Venice.

'Made out of the bark of mulberry trees,' said Messer Nicolo.

'This Khan is a clever magician,' said Marco, smiling. 'I see that he can turn the bark of trees into gold!'

But he looked rather sadly at the yellow notes.

'Cheer up,' said Hans, waving that crumpled old yellow note that had travelled all the way to Venice and back. 'When we get to Kambalu, I'll treat you all to bird's-nest soup.'

'Not for me,' said Tonio firmly.

'Sharks' fins, then,' said the German, 'or bamboo sprouts and rice and ginger and fat ducklings. Or would you like a tender boiled puppy? Don't say no; they're delicious. Or fruit. I'll buy you a nice little pear that weighs ten pounds! Only just a size smaller than your head, Tonio, and much yellower.'

'I'd like a fourpenny loaf from the baker in the Piazzetta,' said Tonio, 'and some ripe olives.'

'I don't see that foreign travel has broadened your mind at

all,' said Hans disgustedly, shoving the old note with the new ones back into his pouch.

They travelled swiftly now. There were fresh horses at the posthouses. The roads were paved with stone. Great trees had been planted along them for shade. The horses went swiftly with their feet ringing on the hard roads. Everywhere Kublai Khan's golden tablets brought people who bowed down before the Polos and helped to speed them on their journey. The news of their coming went on before them, carried by the runners with the bells at their girdles. They ran day and night with the message.

The Khan sent his people a forty days' journey to meet the Venetians. He sent his elephants to carry them over the last part of the road.

Tonio felt dizzy swaying about beside Marco in a gold-trimmed house on the elephant's back.

Tonio said: 'Let's see, there was the boat—that was pretty bad. Then horses: ever so many different horses, big and little. The best was the pony Barka Khan gave me: the one I rode when I didn't hit the apples. The donkeys and asses up and down the mountains. And camels across the desert. They used to make my head go round. But I think this elephant is worse than any of them. I don't like to look at the ground.'

'Then don't,' said Marco sensibly.

'I think,' said Tonio, turning rather pale, 'that perhaps I'd better have a horse at the next posthouse. I hope it comes soon.'

Fortunately the posthouse came in time.

Tonio climbed down a gilded ladder and rode happily with Pietro on a shaggy Tartar pony much like the one Barka Khan had given him.

'Elephants are grand, Pietro,' Tonio said, 'but give me a horse any time—unless I could have a gondola. When we get back to Venice, I'll take you out in mine. It's green-and-gold and skims like a swallow. I hope that new gondolier keeps it clean and doesn't go bumping it around.'

The Khan, they learned from the messengers, was not at Kambalu, where they had expected to find him, but at Xanadu. It was north of the Great Wall, a wall that ran, as the Khan's stone roads did, up and down over hills and through valleys and seemed to have no end.

Xanadu was near the mountains. Its walls were sixteen miles around. Inside them seemed to be every pleasant thing that anyone could find—green fields, great trees waving their thick green leaves, cool streams of water running under scarlet bridges, clear pools with fish jumping in them, quiet gardens with peacocks on the walls, and fountains frisking in the sunshine.

'This,' said Marco, 'is the finest place in the world!'

No one contradicted him, or even laughed at him.

Their guides took them to a house near the palace.

'Kublai Khan will welcome you when you have rested,' they were told.

There was a garden with a pool in it. The boys swam in the pool and washed off the dust of the journey.

'Or at least the top layers of it,' Marco said, splashing water in Tonio's eyes.

'You talk as if we hadn't washed for three years!' laughed Tonio, pulling Marco under the water and sitting on him. 'I have if you haven't,' he added, as Marco came up sputtering. 'Hi, let go of my leg!' and Tonio disappeared among the lily pads.

'Stop drowning each other and get dressed!' roared Messer Maffeo. 'Do you think the Khan wants dolphins splashing all over his gardens?'

They put on the clothes they had brought from Venice—the velvet tunics with the gold-embroidered sleeves, the short black cloaks, the velvet caps with the ostrich feathers, the scarlet slippers, the long silk hose.

Tonio's clothes were so tight in the sleeves that he could hardly move his arms. His feet had grown so that he had to curl up his toes in his shoes.

'The only thing that fits is my hat,' he said.

'My clothes are just as bad,' said Marco.

He looked hard into his shield.

'I think my beard shows up pretty well if you get it in a good light,' he said, combing his curly brown hair and turning his head towards the light.

Tonio stroked his chin with pride. The chicken fuzz had really grown into hairs—several of them.

'We're men now, Messer Marco, sure enough,' he said.

Messer Maffeo, splendid in red velvet and cloth of gold with the Khan's gold tablet swinging against his broad chest, walked laughing through the doorway.

'You "men" had better come along, then,' he said.

He spun Marco around, looking him over.

'Very neat,' he said. 'Bella herself couldn't find a spot on you. A few wrinkles, but that can't be helped on a three years' journey.'

Even Hans looked fine, Tonio thought. The little German had bought himself a new pair of red boots and put them on for the first time. They were as much too big for him as Tonio's were too small, and they slapped around his thin legs when he walked. Mar Sarghis wrapped himself up in a long cloak of purple wool, and stuck a high red cap on his black hair.

'Cheerful! That's what I like to see,' said Messer Maffeo approvingly. 'I like a good dash of color. Nicolo, you look as respectable as an old starling! Depressing, I call it.'

Messer Nicolo was all in black velvet. The only bright spots about him were the Khan's gold tablet and his blue eyes that shone in his brown face. His bush of brown beard was beginning to be just frosted with silver.

'He looks all right to me,' said Marco.

Marco was as tall as his tall father now. His honest gray eyes were on a level with Messer Nicolo's bright blue ones as he smiled at his father and laid an affectionate hand on the black velvet sleeve.

Pietro came in wearing one of Tonio's red tunics with the Polo shield on it. He had one of Prince Argon's golden apples around his neck. The old cord was still on it.

'They say the Khan is ready for us,' he said. 'Baron Kogatai is here.'

The Baron was the chief of the Khan's guard. He was outside the gate with a troop of soldiers. Mar Sarghis, Tonio, Pietro, and Hans picked up from the floor bundles wrapped in brocade and velvet. The three Polos followed the Baron through courtyards and gardens to the Khan's own palace. The soldiers tramped behind them.

The palace had a roof of solid red lacquer, 'curved like a dolphin's tail,' Tonio whispered to Pietro, who wondered what a dolphin was.

There was a great crowd of people gathered about the door of the palace. They stood aside and let the Polos' party go through.

Inside, the walls were of marble and gold with paintings of strange beasts and birds.

'This is the finest palace—' began Marco at the threshold, looking at the bright walls.

'Set no foot on the threshold,' the guards shouted, and waved their clubs in the travellers' faces.

'It's enough to frighten you into doing it,' muttered Mar Sarghis, striding over the threshold with his long legs and hurrying after Marco.

Tonio followed, stepping carefully, holding his precious bundle tightly. The hall was a big one with a high ceiling where gold dragons were having a terrible battle. The place was dim after the bright light outside. Blue smoke of incense drifted through the shadows. For a moment it made Tonio think of the golden twilight of the Church of San Marco, but as his eyes grew used to the light, he knew that he had never seen anything like this place. The figures of the queer animals, the throngs of men dressed alike in robes of crimson, the flash of gold at every belt, of jewels sewn on silk sleeves and even on boots, all seemed strange to him. Tonio had seen jewels and splendid clothes in Venice, but nothing like this sparkling of diamonds and pearls and gold.

But stranger than all the new faces was what was going on at the end of the hall. There was an empty space there in front of the gold-and-ivory seat. Tonio knew that the man on the throne must be Kublai Khan. He sat very straight on his gorgeous seat. His robe of crimson was covered thickly with patterns of flowers and vines embroidered in beaten gold and sewn with emeralds and rubies and pearls. He had a curious round hat on his head, with a diamond in the top of it that flashed in the light from the swinging lanterns. The hat looked like a covered dish. The diamond was big enough for a handle. At the Emperor's throat was a jewelled flower as big as a rose, all sparkling with rubies. The Badakshan ruby around Marco's neck looked small compared to them.

The face under the queer hat was kind and sensible-looking, Tonio thought. The black eyes flashed as brightly as the diamond. The Khan did not have one of those flat Tartar noses. His cheeks were red and white, not like a flat shield covered with leather—like Barka Khan's.

Tonio saw the Great Khan bend forward in his chair and look at the man walking towards him. The man had on a black silk robe with embroidered gold snakes squirming all over it. He walked slowly with his hand on the neck of what Tonio called a striped lion. It was really a tiger, but Tonio did not know that. Whatever its name was, everyone in the hall shrank back as it passed. There was a rustling of silk robes, and then everyone was so quiet that Tonio could hear the tiger's soft feet padding on the marble floor.

The tiger went forward, switching his striped tail from side to side. Once he turned his head over his shoulder, and looked back straight at Tonio out of his blazing eyes, opened his mouth and yawned slowly, showing his cruel teeth and arched red tongue. Then he shut it with a snap that set his whiskers quivering and slouched forward.

The man with the snakes on his back stood still, and the tiger walked on alone, while the Khan bent forward watching him. Suddenly the great beast stopped. He crouched as Tonio had seen cats do before they jump on a mouse. Tonio held his breath. No one in the rest of the great hall seemed to be breathing either.

But the tiger did not spring. Muscle by muscle the huge orange-and-black creature bent down. His tail drooped limply on the floor. The gaily striped head dropped on the white paws. He lay there a moment, then sprang up, arched his back and tail and padded forward a little, then bowed himself to the ground as before. He did it four times altogether. The last time his great claws were within striking distance of the Khan's robe.

Kublai Khan never moved, only gazed at the beast. His black eyes sparkled and there was a smile on his red lips.

'You may go, brother,' he said softly. 'I thank you for your courtesy.'

The silence was so deep in the hall that everyone heard him. The tiger swung around and trotted back to his master. Tonio was glad when he saw the last of that long switching tail.

One of the Khan's Barons touched Messer Nicolo on the shoulder. The three Polos moved towards the throne, bending their knees to the ground and bowing low before the Emperor Kublai, just as the tiger had done. Tonio and the other followers went forward on their knees with the bundles of gifts.

Kublai smiled and told the Polos to stand up.

'It does my heart good to see you, gentlemen,' he said in his clear, deep voice. 'Tell me how have you sped on your long journey?'

Messer Nicolo, in a voice as deep and beautiful as the Khan's said: 'We have sped well, indeed, my Lord, since we return and find you in good health.'

'The road was long,' said Messer Maffeo—he was slightly out of breath from so much bowing, but he managed to speak without panting. 'The road was long, but your strength and power brought us safely over it; and we thank you for your favor.'

He and Messer Nicolo laid the gold tablets at the Khan's feet.

'You are both welcome to my court,' the Khan said; and then, seeing Marco, who was standing a little behind his father, 'Who is that young gallant I see in your company?'

'Sire,' said Messer Nicolo, 'that is my son and your true servant.'

'Why, then,' said Kublai Khan, smiling kindly at Marco, 'he is welcome too.'

CHAPTER 14

ROPE TRICK

WHEN PEOPLE used to ask Marco about how the Great Khan received him, he would say in his jolly way: 'Oh, why should I make a long story about it? There was great rejoicing at the court because my father and uncle had arrived and everyone did us great honor.'

Tonio, however, thought it was a very long story, indeed. No one had told him to get up off his knees, and the marble was getting very hard. Besides, he had felt a stitch give way in the back of one of his stockings.

'A nice thing,' he thought miserably, 'to come into the Khan's court in rags.'

At last one of the Barons told him to get up. Tonio did, and his knees cracked so that he thought it sounded as loud as the snapping of a Tartar whip. He walked towards the throne in his tight shoes, wishing he had on a cloak of darkness instead of his short cape.

Of course no one was noticing Tonio. Everyone was talking now, and no one would have known whether every one of the Polos' followers had ten holes in both stockings.

Tonio handed a bundle to Messer Nicolo, who opened it and set before the Khan the precious flask of oil from the Holy Sepulchre in Jerusalem and the crystal goblets that the Pope had sent. The Khan was pleased with them. He held them to the light to see how clear and sparkling they were.

Then Hans came forward with a gold casket, and Messer Maffeo spread out the best of the Venetian jewels in the fine gold settings that Hans and Mar Sarghis had made.

The Khan spoke politely about the jewels, but he seemed even more pleased when he recognized the little round-faced German and the big Tyrian.

'Why, this is more than I could wish for,' he said, laughing, to Messer Nicolo. 'You have brought me my makers of mangonels again. Now it was sad that you couldn't stay and see my soldiers take that city with your machines. Such smashing and crashing as we had! Oh, well, perhaps we'll play some more of those games. And these men can work in gold one day and heave stones through the air the next! Surely there are some clever fellows in your part of the world.'

Then he looked straight at Pietro, who had just opened a roll of Venetian velvets and was handing them to Messer Nicolo.

'That face never saw Venice, I think,' said the Khan.

'No, my Lord,' said Messer Maffeo. 'He came with us from Barka Khan.'

Kublai looked keenly at Pietro.

'And where did you get that thing around your neck?' he asked, smiling.

'In Persia, my Lord,' said Pietro, kneeling down and slipping the cord from around his neck. 'I brought it for you, Sire, if you would take it.'

He laid the golden apple at Kublai Khan's feet.

The Khan picked it up and began to whirl it around his finger by the cord.

'I thank you. Fine apples they have in Persia!' he said. 'How do you pick them?'

'With—with arrows, my Lord,' stammered Pietro.

'Tell me about that apple-picking,' said the Khan to Marco.

Marco told the story clearly and simply.

'So he shot better than Prince Argon, did he?' Kublai Khan murmured when Marco had finished. 'That is my brother's grandson, though I have never seen him. What sort of man is he, this young Prince?'

'Why, he is a fine sportsman,' Marco replied. 'Like a young fawn for jumping. He has hair like red-gold and blue eyes like the sky after rain. He likes raisins and he shoots with his left hand.'

Kublai Khan smiled and said: 'I had heard he was skilled in sports. A beautiful princess from our court, the Princess Bolghana, is his wife. He would be kind, I hope, to a stranger—in a strange land—But, of course, you wouldn't know about that.'

Marco said nothing more. He did not like to say how he thought Prince Argon might treat strangers if they happened to displease him.

'And the other boy, the yellow-headed one. Did he come all the way from Venice too?' asked Kublai.

'He did, Sire, and he, too, has brought you a gift,' said Marco.

Tonio walked towards the throne. He had something in his hands wrapped in a soft piece of blue camel's-hair cloth. He swept his velvet cap off his yellow hair and knelt down before the Khan, laying the blue bundle on the gold step of the throne. One of the Khan's Barons picked up the bundle and opened it. It had Tonio's precious piece of jade in it—the one he had fished out of the river in Khotan.

'Why, that is a splendid gift!' said Kublai Khan, looking kindly at Tonio out of his keen black eyes. 'I shall not forget it. White and vermilion—my favorite jade. I thank you.'

Tonio got up and backed away. A stitch broke in his other stocking, but he hardly noticed it. Kublai Khan really liked the lump of jade—he kept running his fingers over it and looking at the red specks. Tonio did not care how many holes came in his stockings now. At last he had seen the Great Khan.

All that pleasant summer the Polos stayed at Xanadu. The Khan and his court went hunting in the country around. Tonio used to see Kublai riding in his house on the backs of four elephants. The house was built of wood covered with thin plates of gold, with tiger skins on the roof. Kublai Khan sat in it with his falcon on his wrist. When he saw some game he wanted to catch, his servants would lift the roof of the house and the Khan would let the falcon loose. Kublai Khan had so many falcons that they had what Tonio thought was a palace to themselves.

Sometimes the Khan rode on a horse with a hunting leopard crouching on the horse's neck. The Emperor would slip the leopard at a deer or even at a rabbit. He gave the meat to his falcons. They were always hungry.

Although the Khan lived in such a splendid palace, he had not lost his Tartar ways. One of his favorite houses was not a palace fixed in one spot, but a house of bamboo which, like Barka Khan's house of felt, could be moved about and set up in

different places. The bamboo was richly gilded. Gold dragons held up the lacquered roof. The house was held in place with dozens of cords of silk and hung inside with rugs of the fur of sables, the most precious fur in the world.

When the court moved south to Kambalu, the Polos went with it. Before Kublai left Xanadu he always had all his beautiful white mares milked and had the milk thrown on the ground. It was supposed to bring fine weather and good crops. No one but the Khan's family could drink the milk of the mares. They were so sacred that no common person must go near them, even if he had to go half a day's journey to keep out of their way.

The court travelled slowly towards Kambalu, hunting as they went. Marco was amazed when they came to Kambalu.

'This is *certainly* the finest city in the world,' he said.

He did not even add 'except one,' he was so surprised by the miles and miles of great white walls with their high towers at the corners, and the splendid palaces with their roofs shining with bright colors, and the gardens inside the walls. Kublai's banqueting-hall at Kambalu was so big that thousands of people ate there.

Tonio and Marco saw many strange things happen in that hall.

Near the Khan's own table was a stand of wood, carved and gilded, about nine feet square. A great golden jar in the middle held almost a barrel of wine. From it wine was drawn into four smaller jugs. All the Khan's gold pitchers and his big gold cup with two handles stood there besides.

When the Khan wanted to drink, his magicians made the gold cups move towards him without anyone touching them.

'I tell you I saw it,' said Marco. 'I wouldn't tell you a lie. The cups floated through the air right to the Khan's hand.'

'You only think you saw it,' grumbled Pietro. 'Those sorcerers can make you see whatever they like.'

Tonio had seen the cups move too. He was sure Marco was right and Pietro wrong. He and Marco both laughed at Pietro, but that very evening something happened that made them change their minds.

It was a warm, cloudy evening in September, and after supper one of the magicians went out in to the courtyard. Marco, Tonio, and Pietro joined the crowd of people that followed the

tall man in his wide black robes. His name was Kao-Hoshang. He had a little boy with him, a funny fat little yellow-faced boy with slanting eyes. Kao-Hoshang had eyes set in the same queer way and a black braid of hair hanging down his back.

'He's a Chinese,' said Mar Sarghis. 'They are the people the Tartars conquered. This city belonged to them once. So did the city of Sayanfu whose walls Hans and I broke.'

'All alone? Just the two of you?' asked Marco, smiling. 'Don't joke with your elders,' said Mar Sarghis. 'Watch the man now.'

The boy had a basket in his hand. He suddenly began to pull a rope out of it.

Pietro said: 'Now I have seen this trick before. Do what *I* say, Messer Marco. Don't watch the man. Don't look up when he tells you to. Look down and see what you really see, not what he wants you to see. Tonio can look up and see what goes on up above.'

The magician tossed the rope in the air.

'See, now,' he said. 'It's going up, up, up in the clouds.'

Tonio followed the rope with his eyes. It really seemed to be wriggling up there far above his head, like a snake.

'Go up,' Kao-Hoshang said harshly to his boy. 'My knife is at the end of the rope. Bring it down.'

The boy began to climb the rope with the man scolding him all the time.

'Hurry, hurry, lazy-bones, bring me back the knife! Why, he's gone! The little rascal! Gone into the clouds!'

'I've lost the knife, master,' came a small voice from high above their heads in the darkness. 'Don't beat me!'

The magician said angrily, 'Well, I shall have to go up after it myself, I suppose,' and he began climbing up the rope.

Tonio heard Pietro mutter: 'Don't look up!' to Marco.

Tonio himself looked up into the dim sky. He was sure he saw the magician float up among the clouds in his black robes and then disappear into them.

From the clouds came Kao-Hoshang's voice scolding his boy and the boy's voice crying and begging not to be beaten.

'Ah, so you had the knife all the time!' yelled the magician. 'Well, now, I'll use it. Here, I'll cut off a leg and throw it down—now one arm. That's right—now the other. And here goes the head!'

The boy kept on crying. Tonio, with his mouth open, saw the boy's fat arms and legs, and at last his head with his little round mouth still open—and yelling, come sailing down through the air.

Then the magician appeared. He had the knife in his hand.

'So that's what happens to a boy that doesn't mind his master,' he growled, and threw the pieces of the boy over the wall. 'So now,' he said, with a sigh, 'I suppose I shall have to get a new boy.'

He clapped his hands. Through the gate of the courtyard the boy came running in his little green jacket, with his red cap on his head, his slanting eyes twinkling in his small round face, and his short black pigtail slapping on his back.

Everyone began to clap his hands and talk loudly.

Marco patted the boy on the shoulder and put one of Kublai Khan's yellow notes into the little yellow hand.

The boy's mouth opened in a round O. He bowed to the ground and almost rolled over at Marco's feet.

'Now what do you think, Messer Marco?' asked Pietro in a low tone.

Marco said loudly: 'Why, I don't think—I know! There hasn't been any going up or coming down. Nor any breaking nor mending.'

Kao-Hoshang swung around with a whirr of his black robe and scowled at Marco. Then he turned away again, but he stood very still as if his yellow ears were stretching out to hear what went on.

'But I saw it,' said Tonio, in a low voice, glancing at Kao-Hoshang's black-and-gold back. 'The man climbed the rope and threw the pieces of the boy down. I saw it happen.'

Pietro laughed. 'And what did you see happen, Messer Marco?'

'I saw the man's feet all the time,' said Marco, 'and I saw the boy hide under his skirts. After a while the little fellow sneaked out from under them and went out by the door behind us. He had plenty of time to run around the wall and come back when the man clapped his hands. We shall have to look twice in this country before we know what we see. To make a whole crowd of people see whatever you want them to see is a kind of cleverness that I don't like!'

'And do the Khan's cups move by themselves?' grunted Pietro.

Marco laughed. 'Neither can cups fly by themselves nor ropes hang from nothing in the sky,' he said rather loudly.

Tonio saw the magician looking at Marco again with an expression in his slanting eyes that, for Tonio's taste, made him look altogether too much the way he did when he went up the rope after his boy.

'I saw him climb myself,' said Tonio hastily, and was glad to see that the man in black looked a little more pleasant as he swung away with his black robe rustling.

The boys had not seen the last of that yellow-faced man, however.

Chapter 15

ON THE KHAN'S SERVICE

Kublai Khan took a great fancy to Marco. The Emperor liked the young Venetian's frank, honest way of talking. He liked to hear all the things Marco had to tell of the strange countries he had seen between Venice and Cathay.

'I send my Barons on business all through my Empire,' Kublai Khan said, 'but when they come back, all they can tell me is about the errand I sent them to do. That is stupid. I like to hear about the people: how they look; how they talk; how they live. I like to know how the country looks and what grows there. Tell me now about this province of mine called Zardandan, for I have never been there.'

And Marco began: 'The people of that country all have gold teeth. Or rather every man covers his teeth with a sort of golden case made to fit them. Both the upper teeth and the under. The men also put bands pricked in black on their arms and legs. This is how they do it. They take five needles joined together and with these they prick the flesh till the blood comes, and then they rub in black coloring stuff. It is considered a piece of elegance to wear this black band. The men are all gentlemen—in their own style—and do nothing but go to the wars or go hunting and hawking. The ladies do all the business, aided by slaves taken in war.'

Kublai Khan went on asking questions about far-off places and Marco went on answering them for a long time.

Suddenly the Khan said to Marco: 'What is that I see on your chin?'

Marco blushed. 'It's—it's my beard, Sire.'

'Why, so it is!' said the Khan, smiling. 'Now it seems to me that a man with a beard is old enough to do business for me. Few men in my Kingdom have travelled farther or seen more wonders than you. I know that your father and uncle are as honest as any men in the world and I think you are the same. Honest men don't grow on every bamboo tree. Now there is a city of mine where I think the Governor is cheating me about the taxes. I want you to go there and find out what the trade is in that city and what you think the people pay in customs duties and taxes. You are so young that no one will think you know anything, but you have a pair of good eyes in your head. Stay there a month. Learn what you can without asking too many questions. Then come back and tell me what you have seen.'

So Marco set off on his journey and took Tonio with him. Both young men could speak several languages by this time and also read the different kinds of writing used in Kublai Khan's great country. But the great thing about Marco was what the Emperor had seen: Marco always remembered the first line of the Merchant's Rhyme, 'Honesty is always best.' Both he and Tonio had learned that lesson, not only in Venice, but all

along the road to Cathay. Their first errand was done so well that the Khan was pleased with the results of the business. As usual Marco told him about many strange things that he had seen. That pleased Kublai Khan too.

Messer Nicolo and Messer Maffeo were often sent on errands too. Sometimes Marco did not see his father and uncle for months at a time. Sometimes all three travelled together on trading journeys. No one remembered that they had promised Aunt Bella that they would come straight home from Cathay. Venice seemed so small and far away that at times they almost forgot there was such a place. They spoke in the Tartar language so much that even their own Venetian speech began to seem strange to their tongues and ears.

Everyone called Marco 'Messer Marco' now, and spoke to him with great respect. He was made a Commissioner and ruled over a great city in the southern part of Cathay for three years. All this time the Polos were trading and growing rich. Mar Sarghis, too, was sent as a Governor to one of the Khan's cities. Hans stayed at the court working in gold and jewels for the Khan. There was no need for making mangonels now to throw stones against the walls of cities. Kublai Khan was through with wars. His father and grandfather had conquered cities from Kambalu to Constantinople. Their Tartars—or Mongols as people sometimes called them—had ridden on their tough little horses even as far as Russia and Poland, killing people, burning towns, and stealing. Kublai Khan was not fond of killing and robbing. When he was young he had attacked and conquered cities, but now he only wanted to govern his great Empire wisely. Because the Polos helped him to manage his business well, he trusted them and made them rich.

At the Khan's great feasts the Polos stood with the other Barons of the Empire dressed in the splendid robes that Kublai Khan gave them. Three times a year—sometimes oftener if there was some special reason for rejoicing—the Khan gave all the members of the court new clothes—robes of silk sewn with jewels, broad girdles of gold, boots of soft leather embroidered with silver and precious stones. The robes were of different colors at the different seasons, but always the same color as the Khan's own robe. At other times the Polos were dressed in crimson which was the color worn by the Khan's Commissioners. Tonio no longer had to wear clothes too tight for him. The Khan gave him suits the same color as Marco's, only not quite so handsome. Even Hans had new red boots, finer than any he had ever worn. The Polos and their followers did not win the favor of the Khan without making enemies. One was the magician whose trick with the rope Pietro and Marco had seen through. Kao-Hoshang had never forgiven Marco for telling people that the fat little boy had been under his master's black silk skirts all the time he was supposed to be in the clouds at the top of the rope.

Another man who wished the Polos had never left Venice

was a Saracen called Achmath, who was the Khan's Chief Minister. This man did more stealing right under the Khan's nose at Kambalu than any of the Governors of the far-distant provinces where Marco travelled. Everyone in Kambalu who wanted anything had to bribe Achmath in order to get it. Achmath lied to the Khan about the customs duties he collected on the pepper and spices, the rice and silk, that came into Kambalu every day. And he was cruel to the Chinese people—the yellow, slant-eyed people whom the Tartars had conquered.

It was not Marco's business to tell tales about the Khan's Chief Minister. Kublai Khan had never given Marco any orders to take part in affairs at Kambalu, and Marco did not intend to interfere with them. Achmath, however, felt guilty, and he did not like the Venetian's honest gray eyes that seemed to look through his lying face and see what was going on in his cruel mind.

One summer when the court went to Xanadu, Marco stayed behind in Kambalu. He had some business there with merchants from India who were expected to bring pearls and other jewels. The Khan had first choice of all the jewels that came into the country. Marco had been given the task of choosing the finest for the Emperor. If there were more jewels than the Khan wanted, Marco was to have the next chance to buy them. The Polos turned their wealth into jewels whenever they had a chance to buy fine ones. Precious stones were easier to carry than gold, and Marco never really liked a lot of paper instead of money. Even with Kublai Khan's red seal on it, it never seemed quite like real money to him. Those first rubies that Marco had bought in Badakshan now had plenty of companions.

Pietro and Tonio stayed in Kambalu with Marco. It was

Pietro who came to his master with a piece of news that he hardly dared to whisper.

Marco and Tonio were alone in a shady courtyard throwing a ball to each other when Pietro found them. He looked around to be sure there was no one hidden behind the trees and bushes.

'What's all this mystery for?' asked Marco, tossing the ball in the air.

'It's Kao-Hoshang, master.'

'All right. Who's Kao-Hoshang? I don't remember him,' Marco said cheerfully.

'Don't talk so loud, Messer Marco. Kao-Hoshang remembers you, even if you don't know him. But you do know—the man who did the rope trick.'

'Oh, the yellow-faced man in the black nightgown with snakes on it. Well, what does he want with me?'

'Only to kill you, Messer Marco. He is angry because you laughed at him. This year the Khan did not take him to Xanadu. He thinks you showed the Khan his tricks. He is going to poison you.'

'Oh, he is, is he?' said Marco, tossing the ball to Tonio. 'How did you find out this thoughtful plan, Pietro?'

'You know the little boy, master, who hid under Kao-Hoshang's skirts that night?'

Marco nodded, and Pietro went on: 'Well, you gave him money several times. His master beats him and will not let him go, although he is now almost a man. He likes you and he warned me. They plan to poison you and the merchants from India and steal the jewels.'

'They must be crazy,' said Marco. 'The Khan's guards would catch them easily.'

Pietro lowered his voice even more: 'This isn't all, Messer Marco,' he muttered. 'It's only a small part of a bigger plot. There will be no guards. All through the city the Chinese are saying, "Kill the men with beards." They hate the Khan's foreign Minister. They are going to rise against Achmath and the others and take the city for their own. The boy told me. As soon as the men from India come. And just now, as I was coming through a dark street, I heard one Chinese say to another, "There will be no men with beards here next month."'

Marco dropped the ball on the ground. The summer night was hot. He had slipped off his thin silk coat. Now he thrust his arms into the sleeves and stood for a moment snapping his fingers, thinking.

In a moment he said in a low voice: 'I believe you are right, Pietro. I've noticed restlessness in the city these last weeks. Now this is what we'll do. You, Pietro, will ride to the Khan with a letter from me. You'll ride from the posthouse with the bells around your waist. Ride all the way yourself day and night, north to Xanadu. A fresh horse every twenty miles. Do your sleeping as you ride. The Khan will send his soldiers. The Chinese here will be waiting for the merchants to come from India. That's to be the sign for the uprising—is that right, Pietro?'

'Yes, master.'

'Very well. Then Tonio shall ride south and meet the merchants on the way. I had news yesterday that they were already on the canal. They are less than fifty miles away. I'll give you a letter, Tonio, to tell them to go straight to Xanadu. To see the Khan himself and show him their jewels instead of coming here to Kambalu. The Chinese will be waiting for them. That will give more time for the soldiers to come. We must be

quick and get you started, for the great bell will strike and the gates will be shut.'

In the centre of the city of Kambalu hung a big bronze bell. When a man beat upon it at night, the gates were shut and no one was allowed to go through them or even to leave his house.

Marco wrote his letters quickly while Tonio and Pietro dressed for their journey and packed up some food. Pietro took a skin bag with a little sour milk, some grain, and some honey. It was all he would need for the hundred-and-eighty-mile ride to Xanadu.

They hurried through the gates to the posthouse. At Marco's order both Pietro and Tonio were given horses and leather belts sewn all over with jingling bells.

'What will you do, master, while we are gone?' asked Pietro as the keeper of the horses went back into the posthouse, leaving Marco standing with his hands on the horses' bridles.

'Why,' said Marco, smiling, 'I'm going to warn Achmath.'

Tonio groaned.

Pietro gasped: 'Your enemy! He'd never warn you, Messer Marco, if you were in danger.'

'No. Probably not. But he rules here for the Khan. If people kill the Khan's Ministers, that is only one step from killing him. Achmath has ruled badly. He has robbed these poor Chinese and sold their children for slaves. But if he falls, we all fall. Remember the cry was not "Kill Achmath," it was "Kill the bearded men." Even you, Pietro, have a few hairs on your chin. Kublai Khan himself has a beard, though it is thin and getting white. The Chinese mean to kill Tartars as well as Venetians and Saracens when they talk in dark streets about "bearded men." Go now. I'll take care of myself. On the Khan's service! Ride!'

The two horsemen galloped off: one north; one south. The jingling of the bells died out in the hot summer air.

Marco hurried through the dark streets to Achmath's palace. There were shadows in the doorways. Once he heard a laugh and the words, 'The man with the beard walks fast tonight.' He hastened along, not quite running, feeling more sorry for the Chinese than for Achmath. It must be hard, Marco knew, for the little yellow-faced men with the smooth chins to be ruled by Saracens, Venetians, Tartars—never by men of their own race.

'But things will be better now,' thought Marco, 'because Kublai Khan will find out the reasons the Chinese hate the Governor. The Emperor will make everything right.'

In Achmath's palace there had been feasting. The servants were just clearing away the sweetmeats. Achmath—a dark-faced man with a black beard that grew almost up to his cruel eyes and fell far down over his robe of cloth of gold—was playing dice with another Saracen.

The Minister received Marco curtly. He did not offer him refreshment, scarcely looked at him, and kept on rattling the ivory dice in a shaker of jade and silver.

'I should like to speak to you alone,' said Marco, after he had stood for some minutes listening to the clicking of the dice.

Achmath only laughed harshly.

'You swagger in here with your sword in your belt and ask to see me alone! What a fool you must think me! Say what you have to say and get out.'

Marco swallowed his rage and said quietly:

'You have nothing to fear from me, Lord Achmath. The danger is somewhere else.'

He told Achmath in a low voice the rumor he had heard. He said nothing about the merchants or about the errands on which he had sent Tonio and Pietro. There was no use telling what he knew to the whole city. The servants were still clearing the table. Marco was afraid they would overhear what he said. There might easily be some of them who did not love the tall Saracen with the jade box in his hand.

'If you warn Baron Kogatai, his foot soldiers will guard your palace,' Marco said in a voice hardly louder than a whisper.

Achmath only shrugged his broad shoulders and went on with his play.

'Now that you've told us your old women's tales you have our permission to go,' he said, with a foolish laugh. He threw the dice again. 'Beat that, friend, and I'll give you the two slaves I got today,' he said to the other Saracen. 'Twin boys they are. Painters on silk—clever little imps.'

Marco bowed and left the room.

The voice of the big bronze bell clanged loud over the city as he reached his own door. Everyone in Kambalu must sleep now by the Khan's orders. But Marco lay awake a long time, wondering what was going on below the peace and quiet of the sleeping city.

CHAPTER 16

THE FINEST CITY

TONIO CAME back the next day with the news that the Indian merchants were safely turned aside from Kambalu and started on their way to Xanadu.

'Fine!' said Marco. 'Now today I shall not be poisoned! If Pietro has done his errand as well as you, then the soldiers will come and the city will be safe.'

They waited through one long hot day after another, but no soldiers came from the Khan.

'It is a long road,' said Marco. He began to count the miles on his fingers. 'They couldn't possibly get here before tonight. Yes, tonight would be the earliest, Tonio.'

Towards evening a messenger came to the door.

'Lord Achmath orders you to the Khan's palace; Prince Chinkin is there and demands your presence.'

Prince Chinkin was Kublai Khan's oldest son. 'That means

the soldiers have come,' said Marco to Tonio. 'The city is safe now.'

He dressed himself in his crimson silk with its patterns of beaten gold and went to the Khan's palace. There was a crowd of people near the doorway. In the dim light Tonio saw many Chinese faces in the crowd, but not the troop of Tartar horsemen he had expected. There were only the usual guards, some of Baron Kogatai's troops who belonged to Kambalu.

'The Prince must have left his soldiers at the gate,' thought Tonio.

'The threshold! Tread not on the threshold!' bellowed the guards in their ears. Marco had almost stepped on the sacred threshold of the great hall. The lights were dim in the hall.

Prince Chinkin was sitting at the far end of it. He was in riding-clothes with his bow still at his side. The lower part of his face was muffled in a cloth-of-gold scarf. His jewelled helmet was still on his head. It cast a shadow over his eyes.

One of the servants was lighting some candles just in front of the Prince. They dazzled the eyes of everyone who looked towards the throne.

Tonio muttered in Marco's ear:

'I thought the Prince was taller than that. See, this man's head comes only to the bottom of the gold panel. When Kublai Khan sits there, his head comes to the tail of the pheasant painted on the gold. And Prince Chinkin is even taller than his father. That is the Prince's helmet—or one like it—but it's on the head of a short man.'

Marco looked. Tonio was right.

Marco said softly: 'Slip out, Tonio, as quietly as you can. Go to Baron Kogatai. Tell him the Prince is here. Ask him if he expected him. Tell him what you said just now.'

Tonio slipped quietly along the painted wall, strolled towards the door, and went slowly out. When he got outside the palace and away from the crowd, he ran as fast as he could go to Baron Kogatai's house. Fortunately it was not far, and the Baron was just at the door.

'A message, Baron, from Messer Marco Polo. Do you know that Prince Chinkin is in the city? There is a man on the Khan's seat who looks like the Prince, but Messer Marco is not sure. He is dressed like Prince Chinkin, but he is much shorter.'

'Why, how could he be here?' asked the Baron. 'How could he enter the city without my knowing about it? No one has passed the gate.'

He ordered out a company of soldiers and set off for the palace. Tonio ran back ahead of them. The man in the Prince's clothes was still sitting behind the flaring lights, men of the court were bowing before him. In the crowd Tonio saw the yellow face and black dragon-covered shoulders of Kao-Hoshang. Beside Kao-Hoshang was another man in a magician's robes. He was Chen-Chu, another of the Khan's jugglers.

There was a stir at the door. Lord Achmath came through it. He was taller than any of the men around him. The crowd fell apart for him to go through. He walked towards the throne where the man in the helmet sat behind the bright lights with the gold scarf around his chin. His eyes stared at Achmath from under the shadow of his helmet.

Achmath bowed to the ground, walked forward again; bowed and walked forward. The man on the throne did not speak, only watched the Minister's tall figure and cruel, handsome face. Achmath bowed for the third time. The man on the throne snapped his fingers. There was a rustle of silk. Two black figures stepped towards the kneeling man. Kao-Hoshang

had a mace in his hand. He whirled it into the air. As it fell, a sword flashed out of the folds of Chen-Chu's robe, quivered a second above the neck of the Saracen. There was the dreadful noise of steel on flesh. Lord Achmath fell groaning to the floor.

The man on the throne stood up, grasping his bow.

'Kill the bearded men!' he called.

Baron Kogatai rushed into the hall.

'Treason, my Lords! Treason!' he gasped, and shot an arrow straight at the man behind the lights. The arrow pierced the bare throat under the gold scarf.

The man in the Prince's clothes fell forward, upsetting the lights. His helmet rolled across the floor with a hollow clang. The face under it was a Chinese face. There was no beard on the chin under the gold scarf.

'Wang-Chu!' muttered Baron Kogatai, looking down at the dead man. 'Guard the door! Let no one leave the hall!' he called.

Marco and Tonio had already seized Chen-Chu and taken his sword. Kao-Hoshang was wrestling with half a dozen Tartars. His mace banged on the marble floor. Marco's fingers were bleeding from the edge of Chen-Chu's sword. Tonio had a cut on his ankle.

The guards came in and led the two magicians away.

There were Tartar shouts outside the palace and the sound of horses' feet trampling on the stone pavement.

'Pietro! The men from Xanadu!' said Marco.

It was not only the Khan's soldiers. Kublai Khan himself was there. His elephants waved their trunks in the torchlight as the Khan walked down the ladder from his house of gold. With his soldiers behind him, the Emperor walked through the blood-stained hall and sat down on the seat where the dead Wang-Chu had been sitting such a short time before. Kublai Khan looked around the hall at the prisoners, at the dead bodies, at the waiting Barons in their splendid robes. His face was stern as he looked at them all. For a long time he did not speak. At last he called for an account of what had happened.

And the man he called on to speak was not one of the great Tartar Barons, but the young Venetian, Marco Polo.

This is what is written in the old Chinese records:

'The Emperor desired Polo, Assessor of the Privy Council, to explain the reasons which led Wang-Chu to commit the murder. Polo spoke with boldness of the crimes and oppressions of Achmath which had made him hated throughout the Empire. The Emperor's eyes were opened. He complained that those around him had thought more of Achmath than of the interests of the State.'

After the death of Achmath, Kambalu was better governed and Kublai Khan's Chinese subjects were kindly treated. Kao-Hoshang's boy became a magician in his master's place. He moved cups and tossed ropes as well as Achmath's slayer had ever done. Marco was more than ever in the Khan's favor. Pietro and Tonio were both richly rewarded for their help in discovering the plot. Some of the finest of the jewels that the Indian merchants had brought were given to Marco. Kublai Khan would have made Tonio Governor of one of his cities, but Tonio said he would rather stay with Marco.

'He is the head, Sire,' Tonio said. 'I am only an extra pair of arms and legs for him.'

'A fine strong pair!' said Kublai Khan, with a smile. 'Well, stay with him if you like. And you,' he added to Pietro—'you won't leave him and be a captain in my guard under Baron Kogatai?'

'I—I will do whatever my Emperor commands,' stammered Pietro.

'But you'd rather be a servant to this foreigner?'

Pietro nodded.

'Well, I don't blame you. Stay with him, then, both of you. And don't forget, Messer Marco Polo, that I've left you something more precious than pearls—two loyal friends.' He gave bags of gold to Pietro and Tonio, and to each a horse and a splendid saddle with gold on the stirrups. 'When you ride for me again, you must be well mounted,' he said. 'And, Messer Marco, if there is anything you wish, ask it now.'

Marco bowed before the Khan. They were in his most beautiful garden. The ground was flat there, but Kublai wanted a hill, so his gardeners had made one. He called it his Green Mount. It was covered with splendid trees. His elephants had dragged them there full grown.

The Khan sat on a marble bench in the green shadows. Marco knelt on the grass at his feet.

'There is only one thing, Sire!' Marco said. 'My father and uncle are getting old. We are so happy here that a year comes, and before we know it, it's gone. Messer Nicolo and Messer Maffeo wish to see our city of Venice again before they die. If you could send us home, Sire, it would make us happy. I would come back, of course, as soon as I could.'

All the kind expression left the Khan's face.

'You ask the one thing I cannot give,' he said angrily. 'That is a strange way to pay courtesy and favor—to turn your backs on my Kingdom. To leave any traitor that likes to run a sword into my ribs or crack my head with a mace.'

Marco knelt down. His honest gray eyes looked straight in to the Khan's face.

'Surely, Sire, with all the men in your Kingdom, you don't need me or my friends.'

'Did I not need you last night?' asked Kublai Khan grimly. 'And why is it that you want to go on back all those weary miles to that city of yours? What is it pulls you back there? Tell me. Not you, Messer Marco. I know what you will say: "Venice is the finest city in the world." Your friend with the gold beard there, Tonio Tumba. I remember the name. Stand up, Tonio Tumba. Tell me why Venice is better than Cathay. Is it so much finer than our cities here?'

Tonio stood up. 'No, Sire,' he said. 'You have twenty cities bigger than Venice. Your bridges are more beautiful. Your gardens are greener. Your roofs shine with gayer colors. No sovereign in all the world has such wealth and power as you. Venice is only a little town. But it's our place, Sire. The sea goes ringing through its streets all day. The breezes are the coolest there and the sun the warmest. The Doge goes out in his scarlet galley and drops a ring in the sea because the sea is the bride of Venice. And the sea is kind to her master. It keeps out our enemies, it washes our streets. It is our road to the rest of the world. And the city floats on it, like a pearl rising out of the water. Venetians go everywhere that the sea takes them, but they always come back to Venice. You see it's home.'

The Khan shook his head. 'No, I don't see. My home is anywhere that Tartar horse has ever trod: wherever Tartar arrows fly. I could take my palace of cane—as any Tartar might his tent—and where I set it up, there would be my home. But I see this: You are bent on going, and when the right time comes, you shall go. But not now. Not now.'

He looked kind again. The anger had gone from his face. And for the first time Tonio saw that Kublai Khan was growing old.

'Will they be glad to see you in that city where the sea rings through the streets?' asked the Khan, looking at Tonio with a smile. 'You were a boy when you came. Will they know you now, do you think?'

'Madonna Bella will know us. We promised her we'd come home in seven years. She'll know us, won't she, Messer Marco? Even though we are away more than twice as long.'

'Ah! Some beautiful Venetian lady?' asked Kublai Khan.

Marco smiled. 'A lady older than my father—his sister, in fact—who will stay alive just for the pleasure of scolding us when we come home.'

'You found no Tartar ladies beautiful enough for you, I suppose?' said the Khan. 'Would you stay here with a Tartar Princess for your bride, Messer Marco Polo?'

'You've kept us too busy for us to think about brides, Sire,' said Marco, smiling. 'No Princess would want a husband who was in India one day and Persia the next.'

'True enough,' the Khan agreed. 'And I remember now—you have sailed lately through my country to the west. Tell me now of some of the wonders you have seen there.'

So all that warm summer afternoon Marco told the Khan about the lands through which he had travelled.

Tonio sat by the seat on the ground. He was very sleepy. There had been little sleep for anyone in Marco's house those last few nights. Messer Marco's deep voice went on and on. Tonio dozed off. When he woke up, Marco was saying:

'After twelve days' journey you come to a fortified place called Taican where there is a great corn market. It is a fine place and the mountains are made of salt, the best in the world; so hard it can be broken only with iron picks. The people near-by are worshippers of Mahomet, and an evil and murderous people they are. The most evil in the world. They wear nothing on their heads but a cord some ten palms long twisted about. They are excellent huntsmen; in fact, they wear nothing but the skins of beasts, for they make of them both coats and shoes. There are porcupines that huddle close, shooting their quills at dogs and wounding them. The people live in caves which make fine houses...'

Tonio heard a strange noise above his head. He looked up. Tonio was not the only one who was sleepy. Kublai Khan was snoring!

The breeze blew gently among the trees of the Green Mount.

A tame deer wandered through the garden nibbling at the grass. She stopped in front of a marble seat in the shade with her nose quivering and her bright eyes moving over the three figures in the green shadows. An old man with a tired face above his jewelled robe of gold cloth sat on the bench. One of his thin hands was resting on the curly brown head that leaned against his knee. On his other side a man with hair like wire of stiff gold sat with his head on his knees. Neither the two men in crimson silk nor the one in the flashing gold paid any attention to the deer. She came quite close to the brown-haired one, put out a careful tongue and touched the shoulder in its bright silk. Perhaps that is why only the deer heard the man with the curly brown hair murmur in his sleep:

'But after all, Venice *is* the finest city in the world.'

VISITORS FROM PERSIA

TONIO SAID to Messer Maffeo: 'There was a lot of noise and excitement at the gates this morning. A great company of travellers from the west came into the city.'

The court was at Kambalu again, for it was now October. Messer Maffeo looked as fat and jolly as ever, but Tonio saw that there were gray streaks in his black beard. Messer Nicolo's hair was quite white, but his blue eyes were still kind and keen.

Messer Maffeo roared: 'I should think they did make a noise! I can't see why they couldn't be quiet and let honest people sleep. It's a disgrace!'

'Who were they, Tonio? Did you find out?' asked Messer Nicolo quietly.

'No; but the Khan has summoned you to court and I suppose you'll see the strangers there—whoever they are, Messer Nicolo.'

The Polos arrived at the court in time to see the Khan receive the visitors. They were three Tartar Barons from Persia sent by

Argon Khan. They came to tell Kublai Khan of the death of the Lady Bolghana, the wife of Argon Khan, and to ask that Kublai Khan should send another lady of the same family to be Argon's wife. It was the Lady Bolghana's wish, they said, that only a Tartar Princess of her own family in Cathay should take her place.

Kublai Khan received the Persian Barons kindly, and promised to give them an answer in a few days. The Persians were leaving the hall when Tonio whispered to Marco: 'Look, Messer Marco, that is the little man, Coja, who shot against us at Prince Argon's that time. He's scarcely changed at all.'

'That's right,' muttered Pietro, 'he still struts along like a young cock. I wonder if he can knock down gold apples now. I'd like a shot or two with him.'

'So it is,' said Marco. 'I must speak to him.'

Baron Coja remembered Marco and was glad to see him.

'It's a wonder to me that you still live,' he said, 'or that I do either after that journey. There are Tartars fighting all along the road. We scarcely got through alive. How we shall ever get the lady back safely if the Khan sends her, I can't think.'

'You might go by sea,' suggested Marco. 'I have just been on a voyage to India. The Khan has such large ships that it is safe enough travelling.'

Baron Coja gave a shudder.

'The sea—that's worse to me than a valley with a thousand arrows flying in it, but I will tell my friends what you say.'

'No wonder you don't mind arrows, my Lord,' said Tonio, 'you who shoot them so well.'

The Baron sighed a little. 'My wrist isn't what it used to be,' he said, 'and my eyes are much less keen than a falcon's.'

He talked for a while with Tonio while Marco told the other Barons about the route to Hormuz by India.

'My Lord,' said Tonio in a low voice to Baron Coja, 'if you really are in trouble about the journey home, take the Polos with you. They want to go, but the Khan has refused to send them, although he has promised many times that he would. One Venetian like Messer Marco on a ship is worth two hundred of these cowardly Chinese. And he knows the roads through Persia, too, if you have to travel there. The Khan cannot refuse you if you ask him.'

A few days later, Kublai Khan said that his niece, Princess Kukachin, would go to Persia as the bride of Argon Khan. Baron Coja thanked the Emperor and asked that the party should be sent by sea, since the land route was so dangerous.

'And,' he added, 'since I am unaccustomed to the dangers of the ocean, I ask that you send with us three Venetians of whom I have heard much, Messer Nicolo, Maffeo, and Marco Polo, men who can help us on our journey either by land or sea.'

The Khan was unwilling at first to say yes. The scowl that was so seldom seen on his face was there now. However, he knew that he would have to keep his promise to the Polos sooner or later. At last he said grudgingly that they might go.

'Go back to that city of yours that is built on banks of mud,' he said. 'When you have seen it, I know you will come back once more to Cathay. And you will be welcome.'

Kublai Khan never did things by halves. He ordered a great fleet of junks to be fitted up, thirteen of them, some of them with ten sails. He had provisions for two years put on board the ships. He sent splendid presents to Prince Argon and gave the Princess the most beautiful clothes and jewels that could be found.

The Princess was a plump, flat-nosed Tartar girl, seventeen years old. She looked plain and unattractive to the Venetians as most Tartar women did, but fortunately she was gentle and good-tempered.

'If you have to travel on the same ship with people for two years, it's lucky if they're pleasant,' Marco said.

The days before the fleet sailed were so busy that the Polos hardly had time to think whether they were glad or sorry to be leaving Cathay. There was much business to be finished before Messer Nicolo and Messer Maffeo could leave. Tonio saw the brothers night after night bending over their account books. He himself worked over Marco's accounts, for he was Marco's secretary now and managed much of his friend's business.

The last evening of all Tonio saw something strange. Messer Maffeo and Messer Nicolo both sat with needles in their hands mending some rough old Tartar coats that they wore when travelling in bad weather. But Messer Marco had a coat of the same sort flung over his shoulders and was laughing at their sewing.

'I'm as good with a needle as anyone,' roared Messer Maffeo. 'Ouch!'

He stuck his thumb into his mouth and sucked it hard.

'Who's that out there?' he growled.

'It's only Tonio,' said Messer Marco, laughing. 'I dare say he has some sewing of his own to attend to or he'd help you.'

'I'll do my own,' said Messer Maffeo gruffly.

'Mine is finished,' said Messer Nicolo.

He put on the old brown coat, and Tonio thought for a moment that he was back in the Church of San Nicolo looking into the face of the kind Saint. Tonio went into his own room and finished his packing. It was a longer task than packing his bundle of clothes in the Ca' Polo the night before he left Venice. The splendid suits that the Khan had given him made many bundles, besides all the other things he had bought.

'You'll need a whole ship of your own, Tonio,' said Marco.

'And think of what you will have to pay! How much a load from Tauris to Layas?'

'Two hundred and nine aspers,' said Tonio, with a laugh.

The party left Kambalu that next morning. Zaitun, where the ships were waiting, was a long journey from Kambalu. Kublai Khan rode with them for a few miles in his house on the backs of four elephants. Sometimes the Princess rode with him in the little gold-lined room with the gay tiger skins on the roof, but for the last part of the journey it was Marco the Khan wanted beside him. Kublai Khan did not talk a great deal. The old man hardly seemed to listen to Marco's stories about the places they would pass through, although he had asked Marco to tell him about Java and Sumatra and Ceylon.

'There will be another Emperor here when you come back again,' once he said sadly.

'Then I shall not come, Sire,' said Marco. 'I can be the servant of only one Emperor—the greatest in the world.'

Kublai Khan put his hand on Marco's crimson sleeve for a moment, but he did not say anything. And he did not speak when all that great company knelt before him in farewell, only sat quietly in his house of gold like a carved ivory figure with one ivory hand raised.

When Marco looked back for the last time, the four elephants were still standing there like blocks of gray stone. The Khan's figure in its white robes was only a light spot against the gold.

'The light hurts my eyes this morning,' said Marco, rubbing the back of his hand across them.

It would take too long to tell of that voyage home—of hiding from cannibals behind a stockade on an island for five months while the southwest monsoon blew; of storms and pirates; of pearl divers and pepper trees; of crocodiles and cinnamon.

There was sickness among the sailors and many of them died. Two of Argon Khan's ambassadors died, too, but Baron Coja, the three Polos, and the Princess arrived safely in Hormuz after sailing for two years. Tonio and Pietro were with them. Mar Sarghis had stayed in Cathay governing one of the Khan's cities. Hans had stayed with the Khan, too.

'After all,' he said, 'what I like best in the world is to work in gold. Why shouldn't I do it where there is plenty? And every year I'll get a grand new pair of red boots!'

Mar Sarghis emptied a bag of jewels into Messer Nicolo's lap.

'Mountains never meet, but men do,' he said. 'These are from a slave whose fetters you unlocked.'

Hormuz was as hot as ever. The Polos did not stay there.

'This,' said Marco, with a smile at Tonio, 'is the worst city in the world. Let's get out of it before I have to be carried out. Anyone who wants my share of salt fish can have it.'

Bad news greeted the Princess at Hormuz. Argon Khan was dead. There was fighting going on between his oldest son, Prince Ghazan, and Argon Khan's brother, Kiakatu. Kiakatu had seized the kingdom from his nephew, but even he did not dare to do anything to offend Kublai Khan. By Tartar custom the Princess belonged to the dead man's oldest son. Kiakatu Khan took one look at Kublai Khan's golden tablets with the pouncing falcons on them and sent the party north to Prince Ghazan with an escort of soldiers.

They found the Prince's camp near a tree called the Dry Tree. It stood in a sandy desert, the only tree for a hundred miles around, green on one side, white on the other, with a great circle of cool shade beneath it.

One of Ghazan's Barons met the travellers and led them towards the tree.

'The Prince is there,' he said.

There was only one man in the shade of the tree. He was a thin little man with the ugliest face Tonio had ever seen; a low, wrinkled forehead, a nose so flat that it hardly rose above his cheeks, teeth that stuck out, and a sloping chin. He was sitting cross-legged on the ground stitching a bridle. There was a forge near him with a new shield lying on the ground beside it. The man must have been working at the forge because there was so much soot on his arms and face.

'That's the Prince,' one of the soldiers said to Tonio. 'He pounds metal and stitches leather for sport instead of shooting.'

Prince Ghazan jumped up when he saw Baron Coja. He was bow-legged like most Tartar horsemen, almost a dwarf in height. And yet, when he smiled, Tonio liked his face. Tonio remembered Prince Argon teasing the black cat with a golden apple and then kicking it away; or sneering when Marco missed his shot. If Pietro had not shot so well they might all have been in that mud-walled prison still. Tonio thought that probably Princess Kukachin, who after all was no beauty herself, was lucky to have Prince Ghazan, with his kind, ugly face, instead of the handsome, red-headed Argon.

Perhaps someone had told Princess Kukachin about Prince Argon. She seemed quite cheerful about her change of bride-grooms. Prince Ghazan gave her a beautiful tent held up by a gold pole and hung with wonderful silks. Princess Kukachin settled down to living in it as if she had never lived in a palace in Cathay. Like Kublai Khan, wherever Tartar horses trod or arrow flew was her home. But there was sadness in the camp after the wedding was over, when the Polos went away. The Princess cried when the three Venetians left, and the Polos were all sorry to say good-bye to her. They felt sad, too, for another reason. Messengers had just come to tell the Prince that Kublai Khan had died. Prince Chinkin had died, too. Prince Timur ruled in Kambalu. They knew Prince Timur, and they all knew that they would never go back to Cathay again.

Prince Ghazan loaded the Polos down with presents and sent an escort of two hundred horsemen to carry the rolls of gorgeous silks, the spices, and the gold. He gave to Marco a wonderful sword with three blades that he had forged with his own hands, to Tonio a bridle of his own making, to Pietro a quiver full of arrows.

Princess Kukachin, with tears running down her face, pushed something into Marco's sleeve.

'Take care of him,' she said. 'He will be company for you.'

Marco felt something squirming in his sleeve. It was a tiny gold-colored dog with big round eyes and a tail like a bunch of soft feathers. The Princess had brought him from Cathay.

Marco said: 'I can't keep him, Princess. You will be lonely without him.' But the Princess would not take the dog back.

'His name is Xanadu. Take him to Venice,' she said. 'Someone will like him there.'

That day, when they were riding in the desert with the little dog curled up in a bag on Marco's saddle bow, Marco said suddenly to Tonio: 'I've kept my promise to Donata, Tonio. I've got a dog for her. You promised her a cat, but you haven't got it.'

'Donata? Who's that?' asked Tonio. It took him some time

to remember the little red-haired girl that Marco had pulled
out of the canal.

'She's probably married with a family of children by now,'
said Tonio, 'but, anyway, I'll take home a kitten. I'll get one
in Tauris.'

The kitten that Tonio bought in Tauris might have been
the sister of the one that Argon Khan teased with the golden
apple so many years ago. Her eyes flashed yellow and green,
her ruff stood up around her neck like black thistledown, her
whiskers were as stiff as steel wires. Her paws were black velvet; her tail a waving black plume. She turned out to be a fine
traveller, and often, as they trotted along through Persia, sat
on Tonio's shoulder.

Travelling west from Tauris was easier than when the Polos
made the journey eastward. The roads were better, and there
was no fighting going on in that part of the country. Their
party, with their guard of Tartar horsemen, kept all robbers
safely off their track. They had Kublai Khan's tablets with the
hawks on them and two of Ghazan Khan's with pictures of
lions, besides two plain ones from Kiakatu Khan. There were
plenty of horses to carry all their goods—the presents Prince
Ghazan had given them, the splendid robes that they had
received from the Emperor in all those years, the queer things
that Marco had collected in his travels. Perhaps no caravan had
ever carried so many strange things: the hair of yaks, musk
from the musk deer, crocodiles' teeth, silkworms and mulberry
leaves, seeds of rare plants, jars of sugared ginger, feathers of
all colors of the rainbow, thin cups of porcelain, and dishes
of scarlet lacquer. Marco himself could hardly tell where all
the things came from.

Somehow they were all carried safely to Constantinople—

the bales of precious goods, the chests of clothes, even the dog Xanadu and the kitten that was now bigger than the dog. Tonio called her Kukachin—out of compliment to the Princess, he said. Besides he thought it was really a better name for a kitten than it was for a Princess.

At Constantinople they heard that the oldest of the three Polo brothers, Marco, the one for whom the younger Marco was named, had died several years before. There was no ship belonging to the Polo family ready for them at Constantinople. No one at Constantinople knew them. The men who now managed the Polos' warehouse there looked in surprise at these bearded men who claimed to be part owners of the business. The men at the warehouse were young. They had been there only a few years. They had heard of Messer Nicolo and Messer Maffeo, but they also had heard that the brothers had died long ago somewhere in the East. They did not exactly accuse the Polos of lying, since they came with a shipload of goods and tablets of gold about their necks, but none of the merchants really believed what the Polos said. Messer Nicolo had to hire their passage to Venice in a strange galley.

'They'll learn better before long!' roared Messer Maffeo as he boarded the galley. 'Things will be different in Venice.'

CHAPTER 18

STRANGERS IN VENICE

'GIOVANNI HAS some queer passengers,' said one gondolier to another as a gondola with five men in it whisked up to the steps of the Piazzetta.

The men who got out of Giovanni's boat and who stood gazing about the square were certainly a strange sight to Venetian eyes. They all wore shabby brown robes of a queer cut, although the late summer evening was too hot for such heavy clothing. Their headgear was queer too. One of them had on a turned-up straw hat; another a cap like a covered dish with a button on top. Their leather boots with patterns of tarnished silver were like no boots ever made in Venice. No Venetians wore such manes of hair nor such flowing beards. What could be seen of their faces was tanned to the color of an old saddle. The one without much beard was certainly a Tartar, with his wide, flat face and eyes that seemed to have no lids. As for the others, the gondoliers could not tell from what country they came except that they were evidently foreigners, for they spoke in a tongue that no one understood.

They moved off towards the Church of San Marco after telling the gondolier to wait. The man who spoke to Giovanni seemed to know the speech of Venice, although he spoke it slowly as if he were fumbling for the words and with a strange rise and fall to his voice.

'What sort of fare do you expect to get from those old bundles of rags, Giovanni?' asked one of the gondoliers as the little group entered the church.

'You must be feeling generous today. Do you take passengers for charity?' called another, laughing.

'I'm not worrying about that,' Giovanni said calmly. 'When a man stops at the Church of San Nicolo with a gold cup stuck all over with jewels in his hand, plunks it down on the altar there, and comes strolling out, making no more fuss than you would if you'd lighted a candle the size of your little finger, I don't expect he'll cheat me out of a few bits of silver.'

'Which one did that? The old white beard who looks like San Nicolo himself? Or the jolly old Turk with a voice like a mad bull?'

The gondoliers gathered around Giovanni, all talking at once.

'No. The one with the straw stack on his chin. The others just shoved gold into the priest's hands till he bowed as if the Doge himself were speaking to him,' Giovanni answered.

'They're robbers, perhaps, buying forgiveness for their sins,' suggested one of the gondoliers.

'Now, what do you think they'll leave on San Marco's altar?' asked another.

'Sh! They're coming,' said Giovanni.

The five men got into the gondola again.

'Canal San Giovanni Grisostomo,' said the one with the long white beard, still with that queer accent. 'Then turn into the Rio San Marina; stop at the steps near the corner,' he added slowly.

None of the passengers spoke as the gondola turned and twisted among the other boats on the Grand Canal. It was getting dark, and the lights were beginning to show in palace windows and to quiver in the water below. The lamp in the bell tower was lighted and shone high above the city—almost as high as the stars that twinkled in the sky and in the water all at once. There were horns and flutes, the thump of drums, the ringing of bells, people whistling. The smell of flowers blew out of gardens and the smell of fish being fried in olive oil blew out of kitchens. The water slapped along the smooth marble steps. The tide was coming in and bringing the cool air of the Adriatic with it in salty puffs. Spires and towers and domes were dark against a sky like silvery blue velvet.

'Didn't I say it was the finest city in the world?' murmured one of the men in the shabby brown robes.

No one contradicted him. The gondolier shouted 'Stalé' and swung into the Canal of San Giovanni Grisostomo.

There were no lights along the arched front of the Ca' Polo.

The fat man with the gray beard boomed: 'Too lazy to light the lamps!'

The older one said gently: 'The family may be on the other side of the house or out on the water, perhaps, Maffeo.'

The gondola stopped at the steps to the courtyard, the very steps from which, Tonio remembered, the little girl with the red hair had fallen into the water. The Polos got out. Marco poured so much silver into the gondolier's hand that the man stood there with his mouth open, staring at the shabby figures in their brown coats as they vanished into the shadows of the courtyard.

There were no lights burning on this side of the Ca' Polo either. A dim lamp from a doorway across the court threw enough light on the new iron gates across the stone archway to show that they were locked.

Tonio banged and rattled at the gates. Nothing happened.

'It couldn't be the wrong place, could it?' he said doubtfully.

'Nonsense,' said Marco, pointing up, and Tonio saw in the dim light above his head the Polo starling carved in the stone, the cross with the flowered circles at its ends, and the birds around the archway.

Tonio rattled some more. People began to come out on balconies of the other houses around the court. At last slow feet came thumping down the stone steps of the Ca' Polo.

An enormously fat man with a yellow face stood inside the iron gates: he had a torch burning in an iron holder in one hand. He yawned and rubbed his eyes with the other fat fist. When he moved his hand, Tonio saw that there was a purple scar curved like the Grand Canal on this man's yellow cheek.

'What do you want at this time of night?' said the steward. He had a steward's chain around his fat neck. 'What sort of time is this to wake honest folks up? If you have business with the warehouse, come again tomorrow. And come to the back door where you belong. The city has free places for merchants to lodge and you'd better go there. There's a good one for Turks just a short way off.'

Messer Maffeo was the first to find his tongue.

'Turks, indeed! Open that gate!' he bellowed. 'What do you mean, you fat rogue, keeping the owners of the house standing outside? The back door, indeed! Here am I, Maffeo Polo, and here is my brother, Messer Nicolo Polo, come back from Cathay with his son Marco, and all left to push our noses against the gates of our own house!'

The yellow-faced steward snorted scornfully.

'Oh, so it's Messer Nicolo Polo come back again! And I suppose you pretend you're old Maffeo. Well, now, I can tell you that we've had just about enough of that sort of nonsense here. Messer Nicolo and Messer Maffeo died in the East a good ten years ago. As for you, fatty, you're the seventh beggar that's come here in rags trying to pass yourself off as the owner of this house. Try some other game. That one's stale. You can't even speak like a Venetian!'

He turned to go back up the steps.

'Look here, Luigi Rosso,' said Tonio loudly.

The steward almost dropped his iron torch. He turned, scowling, and came back to the gate.

'Who's making free with my name?' he muttered.

'So it *is* your name, is it?' asked Tonio. 'And where did we poor beggars learn that, I wonder!'

'Why, you could learn it anywhere on the canals,' said Luigi angrily.

Marco strode up to the gate.

'And does everyone know how you got that scar on your cheek? And is there anyone else who can tell just what it cost to cure it at the hospital, Luigi Rosso?' he asked calmly, with his keen gray eyes on the steward's face. 'Open that gate, or you'll be sorry. Where is my brother Maffeo? Where is my Aunt Bella and my cousin Felix Polo and the rest of the family? Come! We've had enough of this.'

Luigi talked less loudly now.

'The family are all away at their castle in the country, fifty miles from here. Young Messer Maffeo has gone for the hunting and the others are with him. I could not let you in while they are gone. I might lose my place,' he muttered.

'Your place, as you call it, will not be worth much if you don't let us in,' said Marco, with a short laugh.

Messer Nicolo said quietly: 'Let us go, Marco. This man is only doing what he thinks is his duty. We can go and stay at an inn and send a messenger to young Maffeo and wait till he comes home.'

Marco said: 'He knows us perfectly well, father. It's spite that makes him keep us out, but he'll pay for it.'

Messer Maffeo roared: 'All very well for you, Nicolo! I am not going to be turned out of the house that you and I bought with our own money. Surely there is someone in the neighborhood who knows us.'

By this time a crowd of people from the houses on the court had gathered around the travellers.

'Who is the Doge?' shouted Messer Maffeo. 'Who is the Lord Admiral? Who are the members of the Council?'

People told him the names, but they were all strange to him. The men he had known had died. New ones he had never heard of had taken their places.

'Let us go, Maffeo,' said Messer Nicolo. 'I am tired, and it can matter to us very little where we rest tonight after all these years.'

They were turning to go when a voice behind them said:

'Gentlemen, I beg you not to go. Sleep in my father's house tonight. My father is Giacomo Loredano. He is away, but I know he would wish it.'

Tonio thought he had never seen anyone so beautiful as the lady who had spoken.

She was dressed all in white with a cap of pearls on her hair. The hair was like wires of red-gold. It hung down over her shoulders almost to the golden girdle at her waist. Her eyes were like the Adriatic on a bright morning.

Marco Polo looked at her a minute. Then he smiled and walked over to her.

'Why, Donata,' he said. 'I've brought you your puppy.' He pulled the lump of silky golden fluff out of his sleeve and put it into the girl's hands. 'Do you remember me?' he asked, smiling down at her with his gray eyes shining. 'You promised never to forget me.'

Donata said softly: 'I haven't forgotten. You pulled me out of the water. Your name is Marco Polo.'

Luigi Rosso changed his mind about opening the gates of the Ca' Polo when he saw the shabby men in the rough Tartar coats being invited into the palace of Giacomo Loredano.

Luigi threw the gates open with a clang and stood bowing at Messer Maffeo's elbow.

'I have perhaps made a mistake,' he stammered.

'You certainly have!' roared Messer Maffeo. 'So you've found out which side of your bread has the cheese on it, have you?'

'There are rooms in the warehouse where my master entertains strange merchants,' said Luigi. 'You could sleep there—since the rest of the house is shut up,' he added hastily.

'He still believes we are beggars!' Messer Maffeo shouted. 'Only just in case we shouldn't be, he'll do us the courtesy of locking us up in the warehouse for the night. How do you know we wouldn't steal the three ducats' worth of salt fish you've got in there, master steward? Now I'm beginning to like this rogue! He wants to run along with the deer and go yelping after his heels with the hounds. I like to see such a clever man. He'll be able to tell his master—who is just my little pink-faced nephew and named after me and no more the master of this house than Tonio there—that he kept the wicked robbers shut up safe. And just in case we happened to be the owners of the house, he'd like to be polite to us. What a position for such an honest steward! Ho! Ho!'

Marco had been talking quietly with his father and Tonio while this outburst had been going on.

Now he put his hand gently on his uncle's shoulder.

'The man can really be of help to us, Uncle Maffeo,' he said. 'That is, if you don't blow him into the canal first and drown him. See here, Luigi Rosso. You know me as well as I know you, but there are plenty of people in Venice who will think we are liars. I am going to show them we are not. We'll sleep in your merchants' rooms tonight. I know that we'll find better beds to sleep on than most between here and Cathay. Bar the doors if you like. Tomorrow or the next day we'll give a great feast here and invite all our old friends to come to it. It will be strange, indeed, if no one of them knows us for what we say we are—the owners of this house. Send for my brother. When he comes home, he can throw us into the canal—if he doesn't like us.'

Then he turned and bowed to Donata. In spite of his shabby, clumsy clothes there was something about that bow that made a woman in the crowd whisper: 'What a fine man he is! I believe he's Messer Marco, indeed. Just as he said.'

'We thank you, Madonna,' said Marco, 'for your kindness. Courtesy counts most when you need it most. Good night. Keep the little dog for me. His name is Xanadu.'

The five figures in the brown coats walked through the arch of the Ca' Polo and the iron gate clanged behind them.

CHAPTER 19

TARTAR COATS AND VELVET GOWNS

OF ALL the busy days that the Ca' Polo had ever seen the next two were the busiest. Boat after boat unloaded supplies under the arches of the warehouse. Gondolas flashed back and forth carrying messages of invitation to the great families of the city. From the bakery, the pastry-cook's, the fruit and vegetable sellers, the butcher's, the fishmonger's, came an endless stream of food—the fattest chickens, the juiciest melons, the ripest peaches, the crustiest loaves. In the big kitchens there was endless pounding and stirring and beating. There were golden streams of olive oil, sticky clusters of raisins and figs, dozens of eggs, pounds of honey. Over everything steamed clouds of spicy air: cinnamon, cloves, allspice, pepper, ginger, nutmeg—all the flavors that had travelled half around the world to season the Polos' feast.

In the banquet hall servants were hanging the walls with the splendid silks that the travellers had brought home. Dragons and queer birds embroidered in gold sparkled in dark corners. On the long tables were thin plates of porcelain—plates so thin and easily broken that they were more precious than the silver bowls and as precious as the gold cups beside them. There were goblets and dishes of Venetian glass, new patterns that the Polos had never seen before. There were silver and gold spoons, gold pitchers for rosewater, and napkins of the finest linen damask from Holland.

Through all the bustle and noise Marco Polo moved calmly about, giving orders and words of praise, and getting smiles in return for both. At his heels followed a small golden fluffy dog with a tail like a plume and eyes like dark topazes. The dog was attached to a silver chain. The other end of the chain was in the hands of the girl with the red hair. The black cat—Kukachin had grown to be a cat the way kittens always do—sat on Madonna Donata's shoulder and tickled her new mistress's cheek with her silky black ruff. Sometimes Kukachin jumped down and tried to find where that wonderful smell of frying chicken was coming from. Sometimes she spat at the little dog and made him rush at her with small Cathayan yelps. At others she arched her back beside a white marble staircase, waved her black feathery tail, and sang in Persian. Whatever she did she got plenty of attention and someone with gentle fingers to tickle her behind her fringed ears. Kukachin liked Venice. She purred in her own tongue: 'This is the finest city in the world.'

Xanadu was more polite. 'This is the most beautiful lady in the world,' he barked in purest Tartar, but not even Messer Marco Polo understood him.

The guests who came to the Ca' Polo that night were received, not by bearded men in rough brown Tartar coats, but by three splendid-looking gentlemen in long robes of crimson satin that reached the ground. The best barbers in Venice had shaved their beards and cut off their long hair: and had told stories to everyone else in the city about how long those beards were!

When the guests were all seated at the tables and water had been served them to wash their hands, the Polos went out, took off the robes of satin, and came back into the banquet hall again in robes of crimson damask. They ordered Pietro to cut up the robes of satin and divide them among the servants.

After the hosts had eaten some of the good things, they went out again and came back in suits of crimson velvet. Then Tonio cut up the crimson damask robes and gave them to the servants. When dinner was over, the Polos came back in some of those splendid robes of silk, stiff with jewels and beaten gold that the Khan had given them. The crimson velvet robes were cut up and given away.

Tonio and Pietro, too, were dressed almost as handsomely as their masters. Plenty of the people sitting around the table would have liked a piece of one of their robes if it had been cut up and given away.

At last the tables were cleared. All the Venetian servants left the hall. Marco got up from his place at the table.

'Get some sharp knives, Pietro,' he said, 'and bring them here.'

With Tonio's help Marco carried in the worn old brown coats and laid them down at one end of the table. He took one of the coats and began to rip it along the seam. Everyone in the room was so silent that you could hear the thread squeaking against the knife. There was a tinkling sound. Stones rattled down on the black oak table—stones that blazed red and blue and green in the light of the candles.

Someone gasped, but no one said anything for a moment as more and more stones were poured onto the bright heap, and the knife went on ripping the threads.

Then people began to talk louder and louder, faster and faster, while diamonds and pearls rolled out on the black oak.

At last they were all there—such a blazing heap of treasure as no one in the room had ever before seen tumbled in one pile.

Marco put down the knife and said quietly:

'I think that some of you gentlemen were not quite sure that my father, my uncle, and I were really Nicolo, Maffeo, and Marco Polo. We don't blame you. We know that we have all changed; that even now we speak our native language not just as people do who have always lived in Venice. We have taken this way of showing you that at least the three men who claim to be the Polos are not beggars.'

An important-looking old gentleman at the end of the table said firmly: 'I never had the least doubt about your being the Polos.'

Said another: 'Even if I hadn't known your father, I should have known *you*, Messer Marco. You are a true Polo. Every inch of you, like your brother, only taller.'

'And so much handsomer,' whispered one of the women loudly.

'It's fine to see our old friends again,' said a third man. 'How we have missed you, all this time!'

'You must come to dinner at my house, Messer Marco, and tell us your adventures. My daughters will enjoy them,' smiled a plump lady in a red-and-black gown.

Marco made polite answers to all his guests, but to Donata he said with a smile: 'You knew me when I was still wearing my old coat.'

'Tell us about the Great Khan,' called a voice from across the hall.

'Yes, Messer Marco, tell us all about him,' chimed in many others.

Marco stood up with the candlelight shining on his jewelled robe and striking colored flashes of red and green and blue fire from the rich heap in front of him.

'Why, Kublai Khan,' he said, 'was the richest man in the world—and the wisest. We are all proud that he was our friend. He had millions of subjects, millions of gold ducats a year to spend, millions of wealth in jewels and fine horses and grand palaces. But if he had had only a Tartar tent to live in, he would have been a friend worth having.'

Marco was silent a minute. The questions began again.

'Where is his home? Where is this Cathay, then? What was so wonderful about this heathen Tartar?'

'His house,' said Marco, 'was wherever Tartar arrow whistled or wherever Tartar horses trod.' He paused again a minute, thinking of the Green Mount and the Khan's kind voice. 'If heathens are generous and loyal and wise, then Kublai Khan was a heathen. Some day I will tell you more about him, but tonight—'

Downstairs in the Ca' Polo the iron gate clanged. There were people's voices, loud voices on the stairs. Marco stopped speaking. Tonio heard the important old man at the end of the table say to his neighbor, 'Millions! What does he mean by millions? What stories he tells!'

'Marco Millions!' the other said, with a chuckle.

Marco heard him, but he did not mind. He did not feel like talking about Kublai Khan. to all those people just then. He was thinking of the old man in his house on the elephants' backs,

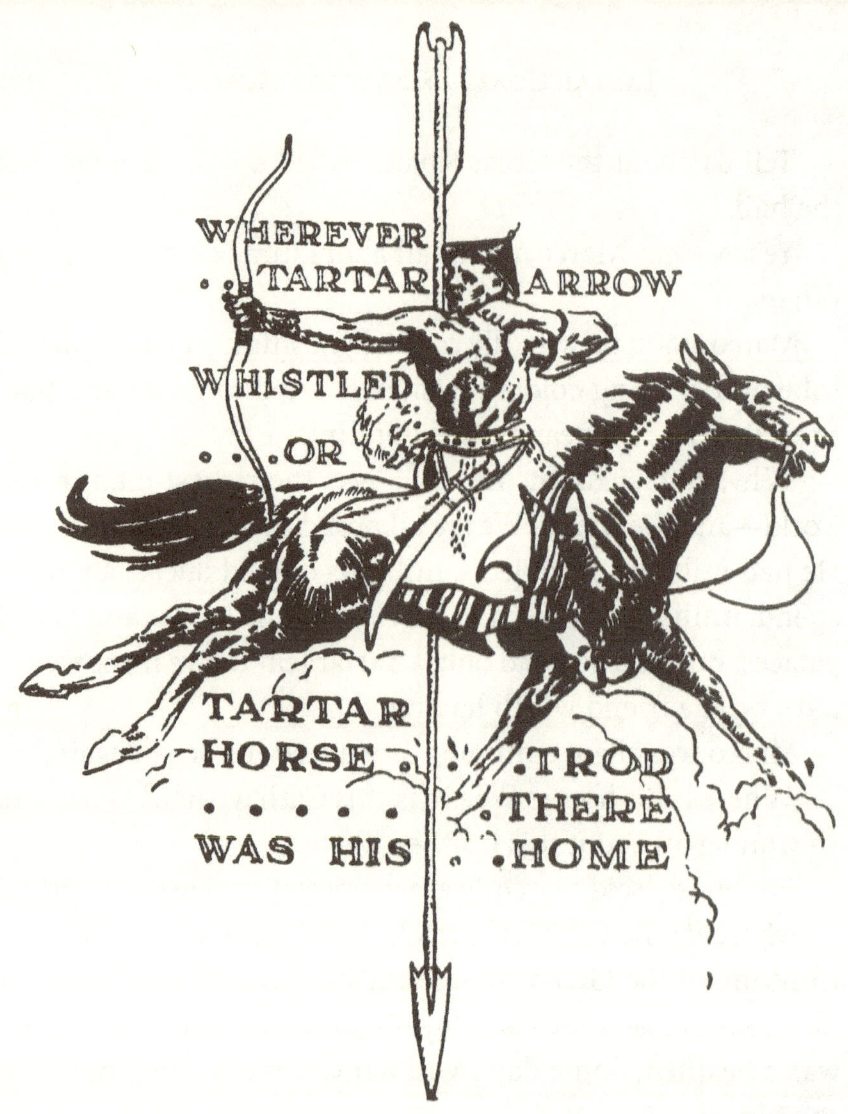

holding up his hand. The voices on the stairs grew louder and people in the banquet hall began to talk again.

'I think I know that voice,' said Messer Maffeo nervously.

People began to rush into the room. The loudest, shrillest voice of all said: 'Maffeo Polo! Where have you been all these years?'

'To Cathay, my dear Bella,' said Messer Maffeo. 'And don't you go scolding us about it. We came back as soon as we could. And look what we brought home!'

The sight of the pile of jewels in front of Marco made the meeting of the various members of the Polo family a pleasant one.

'How much do you suppose they are worth?' asked young Maffeo of his brother. Young Maffeo was no longer a pink-faced boy, but a practical red-faced man rather like his Uncle Maffeo, with a smaller-sized voice.

'Oh, a million, I dare say,' said Marco carelessly.

Someone behind him laughed and said 'Marco Millions' again.

Aunt Bella saw Tonio and shrieked: 'Saints preserve and help us! If here isn't that Tonio Tumba! Well, I suppose you want a job as gondolier. I'd better tell you right off I haven't any suit big enough for you.'

'Tonio isn't a gondolier now, Aunt Bella,' said Marco. 'He's my secretary and partner.'

'Secretary, indeed!' sniffed Aunt Bella. 'Marco with a secretary! I never heard such nonsense. Why, I rapped your fingers for stealing candied ginger out of my cupboard no longer ago than *that!*'

She snapped a thin pair of fingers under Marco's nose.

'I've brought you some ginger to make up for it, Aunt,' said Marco, laughing. 'All the way from Cathay.'

'About time you did,' grunted his aunt, and began to scold Messer Nicolo, who up to this moment had escaped her notice.

'What a lot of pretty cousins I have!' Marco said to Donata. 'Now who is the one in the yellow dress and the brown curls tumbling down her back?'

'That's Rosa, Felix Polo's daughter,' said Donata. 'Do you like brown curls?'

'Why, yes,' said Marco. 'Not as well as some other colors,

though. Tonio, that's Rosa Polo: the one you chased with half a dead eel one day. You ought to go and speak to her.'

'And remind her of that?' asked Tonio.

'No, of course not! Tell her what a big man you were in Cathay.'

'But I wasn't,' said Tonio. 'At least not very. Not like you.'

'Never mind,' said Marco. 'I shan't give you away. You're going to be one—in Venice.'

Tonio became an important man in Venice just as Marco said he would. He never forgot the words of the Merchant's Rhyme that he and Marco had learned, kicking their heels above the water of the Canal San Giovanni Grisostomo. He was honest, courteous, and generous and he became one of the rich merchants of the city. His ships and Marco's—for they were partners always—travelled to the East and brought home the silks and spices that they sold not only in Venice, but to all the other countries of Europe, and even to the distant island of England on the edge of the Atlantic. No one could ever fool Tonio on the amount it cost to bring a load of silk from Cathay. He could count over every asper that had to be paid. He never forgot to share his wealth with the Church of San Nicolo, or to be grateful to the family that had helped him when he was only a shabby, half-starved boy. He married Rosa Polo—who either had forgotten about that sandy, clammy eel or else forgave him for chasing her with it. You will probably not be much surprised to learn that their eldest son was named Marco!

Perhaps it is not very surprising that Marco married Donata. They had three daughters.

'Much better than sons,' Marco used to say. 'Sons go off to all sort of queer places. Daughters stay at home.'

'You ought to know,' his wife used to say, laughing, and the little girls would beg: 'Oh, father, tell us! *Please* tell us, about the Great Khan. Tell us about when Wang-Chu was killed and you were right there on the spot. Tell how you brought home the rubies for the screen at San Marco's!'

One day Pietro came into the banquet hall and said: 'There are two men at the warehouse to see you, Messer Marco.'

Marco was playing a game with his three daughters, Fantina, Bella, and Morena. Marco was Achmath, Fantina was Kao-Hoshang, Bella was Chen-Chu, and Morena was Wang-Chu. Fantina and Bella had just killed the cruel Achmath with a broom and Marco's old scarlet riding-whip.

'Help me up, Pietro,' said Marco. 'I am getting too stiff in the joints for such games.'

'Pietro will play,' said Fantina.

'Pietro is the steward now and has no time for such non-sense,' said Marco, brushing off his velvet tunic. Pietro was a very important man at the Ca' Polo now. 'I must go to the warehouse. Who are these men, Pietro?' asked Marco, and wiped his hot face.

'Two shabby men from a long way off,' said Pietro.

There was something queer in his voice.

'I thought they had better come up here,' he said. 'I think they're outside. "Mountains never meet," Messer Marco, but—'

Marco's three daughters saw their father run out of the room. They ran after him, of course. Two men in the queerest, dirtiest old coats they had ever seen had their arms around his shoulders.

Marco was thumping them both, and saying: 'Hans! Mar Sarghis! Where's Tonio, Pietro? Where's my father? Where's Uncle Maffeo? Well, find them! Hurry up! Look, Hans, I've got three daughters, and all red-headed. Did you ever see three nicer girls? This one just killed me with a broom. Tell me, Mar Sarghis, how you happened to come.'

'When the Khan died,' said Mar Sarghis, 'Hans and I didn't like it much in Cathay.'

'You know Prince Timur, Messer Marco,' said Hans.

'I know him all right!' said Marco.

'He took my city away from me,' said Mar Sarghis. 'He wouldn't give Hans any gold to work with. He'd hardly give him a new pair of boots. Fighting was all he liked and we've had enough of that. It made us pretty tired, so we got ourselves a couple of camels and came home.'

'Just as easy as that?' asked Marco. 'How long did it take?'

'Oh, about five years,' said Mar Sarghis.

'Six,' said Hans.

'Oh, well! Have it your own way,' said the big Tyrian. 'I don't want you to knock me down!'

Tonio came hurrying up the big stairway. Fat little Marco Tumba was riding on his father's shoulders.

'Hurry up, you lazy old camel!' said Marco Tumba, jouncing up and down.

The 'camel' began to jounce, too, when he saw Hans and Mar Sarghis, and the little boy almost fell off. He didn't see why his father wanted to hug both these rough-looking men at once and talk so loud.

Marco Tumba opened his mouth to howl. He opened it so wide that it looked like a square hole in his face.

The man in the queer red boots said: 'Here, Messer Marco Tumba, I have something for you in my bag.'

He put his hand into a big skin bag without much hair on it and pulled out a bright red ball.

Marco Tumba grabbed the ball.

'I like it,' he said. 'Thank you. I like you, too. What else is there in your bag?'

Tonio laughed: 'You see he's a merchant already. You'll see what's in the bag later, Prince Marcolino Tumblekin.'

'Doesn't anyone want to see what's in my bag?' asked Mar Sarghis.

'We do!' squeaked the three girls.

'So do I!' said Marco Tumba, dropping his red ball.

'Give them some rest now,' said Marco Polo. 'They're not going away. You'll live here, of course. Both of you. Find them some good rooms, Pietro.'

'We shan't bother you, Messer Marco,' said Hans. 'We may look a little shabby, but—'

'I know,' said Marco. 'You've got something sewed up in your coats!'

The three little girls squealed: 'Let us see you rip them up.'

There were plenty of jewels in the coats.

That was a fine day for Bella and Fantina and Morena, and for Prince Marcolino Tumblekin.

One day Fantina asked Tonio what was the finest thing he ever saw.

Tonio thought a long time. He remembered the great cities in China with their scarlet bridges. He thought of the Tartar tents swaying over the plains with the white oxen stamping ahead of them. He could shut his eyes and see Pietro galloping under the golden apples and shooting over his shoulder and the apple falling. He thought of the Khan's great feasts where the sorcerers made the gold cups move and where the tiger came in and bowed at Kublai Khan's feet. His mind seemed to touch snowy mountains on the roof of the world, and green, steaming islands in hot seas.

'Tell me, Uncle Tonio,' asked the little red-headed girl again, 'the very finest. What was it?'

Tonio smiled.

'Why, Fantina, the best thing I ever saw,' he said, 'was the roof of the Campanile shining like a star in the sun. And the domes of San Marco's under it. Because, after all, you know, as Messer Marco says, Venice is the finest city in the world.'